MAMA AND
THE LATHAN'S CAFÉ

CHARLENE LATHAN

Printed in the United States of America

First Printing

ISBN: 978-1-7346100-4-8

This is a work of fiction. Names, characters, businesses, places, events, locales, and incidents are either the products of the author's imagination or used in a fictitious manner. Any resemblance to actual persons, living or dead, or actual events is purely coincidental.

Book published by McWriting Services
Houston, TX
Contact us at: sharon@mcwritingservices.com

DEDICATION

I would like to dedicate this book to James Jr.,
Patricia, Debra, and Doris Jean.

CONTENTS

PREFACE

E veryone wants a "Mama." If you don't have one, you will be seeking substitutes all of your life. This riveting story comes from a "Mama's" perspective when she was employed at Lathan's Café. The wounded adult children in the café became hers simply because there was an apparent lack of genuine love in their lives. The individuals who worked at Lathan's were gifted with this beautiful woman for almost a decade. For some she was the only loving mother that they knew. This book is a tribute to them and the time that they spent with "Mama."

INTRODUCTION

This story tells what happened at the restaurant where I worked starting in 1975. It tells about managers, homosexuals, and how they live, and about the good and bad I encountered there. It was mostly bad, though. I tried to draw a picture for you to see what I saw. I saw kids that were seeking love any way they could get it. I learned that they were good actors and actresses; they acted like they were happy when they were in pain. I learned a lot from the kids, especially how to love. If they were your friends, they were truly your friends. They would do anything for you; they'd stick together and help one another. They were very compassionate and very strong emotionally. I'm glad I had the opportunity to work with them.

I learned that they were good kids, but they were rejected by their parents and society. Their lives were not easy, so that's why they stuck together. They had to because no one really cared about them. I gave them all my love, until I was drained. Some people thought that I was homosexual, but I'm not. I'm just a woman of color, and I know how it feels to be rejected by society. I learned from the kids how to be strong, and there's strength in unity. When you stick together, you are all stronger.

Working at the restaurant, I really had a chance to develop my mind. I was exposed to a lot of things, but I didn't forget my upbringing. I would visit gay bars with the kids, just to see what it was all about. I never let the kids see me do wrong. I never lost their respect; I was always Mama. I would visit their homes, but I would never drink alcohol or smoke pot with them. I was always Mama.

I remember the early days. Looking back after ten years of working at the restaurant, my life was not the same. I felt different. I was a better person. I have learned

how to appreciate things and people more. I learned how to be a manager on the job, how to take care of business, and how to take care of people. It was all in a day's work. I will admit; I went through some tough times at the restaurant. It wasn't all good, and it wasn't all bad. It was more like going to college. I had to learn about other people and how they lived. I learned that every nationality is different in their food, music, religion, and just about everything. We were many nationalities in the restaurant: Iranian, African, Jewish, Irish, German, etc. But we had one thing in common. We felt pain the same, so we became one big family, sharing and caring for each other. We didn't care about race or color. We cared about people. That was the bottom line.

I never fudged issues with the kids. I told them when they were wrong, and I apologized to them when they were right. I didn't like their fast lifestyles, their drugs, or their alcohol, but I couldn't stop them. They were seeking an easy way out—a way that they felt they didn't have to deal with the issues of life—so they drank, smoked, and had sex. Crazy sex. All kinds of sex to ease their pain, but nothing helped them. I would tell them about Jesus and who he was, but they seemed to think it was a joke.

One day Juan asked me, very bluntly, "Is He for real, Mama? How can you get pregnant without having sex? So, how could Jesus be born without Mary having sex?"

I was shocked, but I tried to answer him in a way he could understand, because if you're a person who doesn't read the Bible, and believe in your heart that what the Bible says is true, it's hard to understand when a person tells you what the Bible says. I had to give him an answer, so I said, "Clear your mind so you can understand. If society can take a male sperm from a man in Germany and insert it into his wife's uterus in America, without their having sex, why do you think God can't do that too? I am for real!"

He looked at me in amazement. He didn't know what to say. I was glad I had an answer because I had to stay on top of things. If I didn't have an answer, they would intimidate me. They believed in me, and they respected me highly. They thought I had all the answers, but I didn't, although somehow God would always give me ways to respond.

Every religion was different. Mohammed, the Iranian, believed in Mohammed. The African believed in Buddha. I believed in Jesus and the Trinity. To me there was none other. I remember asking LeJebbe, the African, about his religion and customs. He told me he would never marry an American girl.

I asked, "Why not?"

"Our different religions and our customs," he said. Where I was born, they cut me 24 times." He pulled up his shirt to his neck, and on his left side, he had 24 long cuts in a line starting from under his armpit to his waist. He went on to explain, "That is our tribe sign. Everyone in our tribe has these cuts in their left side, so we know everyone in our tribe. If I marry an American girl, she would never let me cut the baby. So, you see, I could never marry in the United States. I have to marry a girl from the Shibulla Tribe."

I thought that was amazing.

I didn't know that I would learn so much from the kids. Mohammed's customs were very serious. If something was going wrong in his country, all the Iranians would go on a hunger strike and would not eat for days, until the problem was solved. I thought to myself; that was pure loyalty. Americans can't go for hours without eating, and Mohammed went ten days at a time. The last time, he passed out, and we had to take him to the hospital. He was dehydrated and malnourished, and we almost lost him. He only weighed 120 pounds before the fast. After he started going on hunger strikes, he lost weight down to 90 pounds. He looked so bad. I thought he was going to die, but he made it.

We also had a Jewish manager. He was very young, about 25, and his religion was different too. He would fast one day out of the year for all his sins. He didn't believe in Jesus, but he believed in God. We were all different in our religions, but we loved the same. We cared a lot for each other. They all loved me, and I loved them. We realized that there is a million different people, but we have one world to live in, so we had to live together, and at Lathan's Café, we did. We worked together, and we loved each other.

LeJebbe, the African, was here in America to go the University of Houston for his doctorate. He worked at Lathan's Café in the afternoons. His body odor was very strong. He never used deodorant. Buddy, the manager asked him, "Why don't you use deodorant?" LeJebbe explained, that in his country, the man has to be masculine, and if he has no odor, he is not considered a man. Buddy smiled and said, "You must be the king of your country." LeJebbe didn't find it funny.

The next day Buddy went out and bought LeJebbe five bottles of deodorant and put them in the dishwasher's area. Then he went around the corner and peeked back around the corner to see if he would use it. LeJebbe picked it up, read the label, and threw it into the garbage. Buddy saw him and laughed. He shrugged his shoulders while saying, "I tried, but it didn't work."

LeJebbe could clear the dishes out fast. He worked hard, so Buddy didn't want to fire him. We had to walk by fast when LeJebbe was around. We believed he was a man if body odor made him a man! His body odor made our eyes tear up. He smelled like an animal, not a person.

I REMEMBER HOW I GOT STARTED AT LATHAN'S CAFÉ

It was a cold rainy day. I had to go on the north side of town to pick up a guitar for my son.

I stopped at the Shell station to get gas; it was cold. I could smell a food aroma in the air. It smelled like steak—charcoal-broiled steak. It was coming from Lathan's Café. My mouth began to water for a steak, when I saw a sign outside of the window that said "position for manager." I didn't know whether I could be a manager, but I would train for one. I left the gas station and went across the street to check it out. The building was made weird. I knocked on this big brown door, but no one could hear me. The door was locked because lunchtime was over. The manager had locked the door to setup for the next shift. I walked around to the back.

I saw a man putting out the garbage. I asked him if I could see the manager. He spoke very little English, so he nodded his head and said, "Manager."

"Yes," I said.

He beckoned for me to follow him. I went in through the kitchen entrance. There were potatoes, lettuce, and tomatoes all over the floor. I looked around as I followed him to the manager's office. I met one guy. He had long blonde hair and long fingernails and spoke very softly. Finally, I reached the manager's office, which was behind the liquor room. The manager was sitting at his desk with his feet on top of the desk. He had on cowboy boots that needed polishing. He was playing with his beard.

When he saw me, he jumped up and asked, "Can I help you?"

"Maybe," I answered, "I am looking for a job."

"What kind of job?"

"I would like to train for manager."

"That's good," He nodded. "I am in training myself. I will train for three months at this store, and then I will move to a larger store." I noticed that "Jerry" was printed on his nametag. Jerry was very friendly. He gave me a form to fill out and told me to sit in the dining room and fill it out and bring it back when I finished.

I went into the dining room, and the waitresses and waiters were having lunch. They stared at me. The boy that I met in the hallway, when I was on my way to the office, came over to the table where I was, sat down and said, "I am Monora."

I shook his hand. "I am glad to meet you, Monora."

His hands were soft. I felt bad because my hands were so rough. Then he asked me if I was a lesbian. I looked up at him with widen eyes, and firmly said, "No." Then I just stared at him for a while.

"That's okay," he said accepting my response. "I am gay, and most of the people here are too."

I was from a small country town, and in that town, I knew of one sissy. That's what they were called. I didn't know anything about gays at all. The only thing I knew was he was so friendly and nice to me.

After I filled out the form, I went back to the office to return it to Jerry when he asked, "Can you start tomorrow?"

"Yes," I replied.

He gave me instructions: "Don't come to this store. Go to the Gessner store. There is a Black lady name Joyce. She will train you; she is very good. She will train you for two weeks, and then you will return back here at this store."

Jerry also gave me the address to the Gessner store. I was there the next day to train with Joyce. The store was huge, much larger than the one on Shepard and much cleaner.

Joyce was expecting me. She met me at the door smiling. "Are you sure you want to work on Shepard?" I didn't know what she meant at the time, but I found out later. She said, "Mostly gay guys work on Richmond; I would never work there." I just smiled, and so did she.

The north side of town was a real crime place run by drug dealers, rapists, and robbers. The Montrose Strip was about fifteen miles long with bright lights and barren areas on both sides of the strip. Homosexuals would walk all night—up and down the strip. They didn't fear danger, although it was dangerous for them. Some gangs would drive to the area looking for gays just to beat up. People were mean. Even if gays were minding their own business, gangs would pick at them.

Joyce began to show me how to make salad for the salad bar. She brought three boxes of lettuce from the walk-in cooler, which had everything in it. Steaks of all kind—marinated steaks. They did not have a bone; they were all meat. She showed me how to chop lettuce really fast. She was very fast with everything. After we chopped the lettuce, she brought out carrots, cucumbers and onions. Everything was in cases. We chopped and chopped.

I said to myself, "If she can do it, I can too."

It was very hard, though. After we finished making the salad, we washed boxes and boxes of potatoes to bake. We put six pans in the oven at a time. When they finished, we put in six more pans—big pans. Each pan held 50 potatoes. Then we got the bread ready to heat in the bread oven, cupped butter, and cut lemons for tea.

Joyce worked so fast. We started at 8 a.m. By 11, everything was set for lunch. The salad bar was ready. The steaks were ready. The grill was hot, and lemons were sliced. Right before lunch was served, Joyce would garnish plates with one slice of cantaloupe on a head of endive and a baked potato.

We had to make everything fast. Lunchtime was fast paced, and I was running lunchtime. I don't know how I made it, but I did. My first day was hard. The second day was the same routine.

At the end of the week, Joyce said, "You are ready to go to Shepard; you got it."

I was fast. I tried to be faster than Joyce. She was super good, and I could not beat her at anything. We would start at the same time, but she would finish before me. The hardest thing to do was the crab legs. They were very long Alaskan crab legs. We had to cut one leg into four parts, rubber band, and place them into the steamer. Joyce was so fast that she could finish a box full while I was still working on half of a box. After a week I got faster, and I could do a box in the same amount of time as Joyce.

Lobster tails were hard to do at first, but I caught on fast. You had to split the shell of the lobster down the back, pull the meat to the surface, and lay it on top of the shell. To get it ready, it had to be sprinkled with paprika and melted butter, placed on a tray, and stored in the walk-in cooler.

Joyce taught me everything about Lathan's Café. I worked with her for two weeks, and I was good. I knew I was good. The next week, I went back to the north side store; I was ready. I made the salad, potatoes, lobster, crab legs, marinated chicken and club steaks. I could do it all. Jerry, the manager was impressed with how fast I could work. I could do my work and help others with theirs.

The work wasn't hard at the store; it was the kids that worked there. Eighty percent of the staff was gay, which wasn't a problem with me, but it was a problem for them. Their lives were as different as wearing two left shoes. They were men trying to be women, and they told me it was hard. Their lives were hell—especially Andy's. He was a handsome head waiter. He was a hard worker. He could make the lunches go really smooth, but he led a double life. During the day he was a very fine waiter, but at night he was a vampire. During the day he wore good cologne; he smelled good. We became very good friends, but the kid had problems.

At night, he would walk the street, looking for guys to pick up. He would wear cutoff jeans and a body shirt, with open-toed sandals. In his back pocket he wore two handkerchiefs. He told me that they represented what kind of lover you were. If you wore blue, you were just a regular lover, but if you wore red, that meant you were a *fist lover*. In other words, you used your fist to have sex. He wore both handkerchiefs, meaning he went both ways. He was a troubled kid who did not know who he was or what he wanted out of life. During the day was a camouflage to cover up what he really was. He said society wouldn't accept him. If he told them who he really was, then they would look at him like he was dirt.

I didn't have the same problem he had, but I could not help but to feel his pain, as far as how society accepted or rejected you. My reason was not my sexual preferences; it was my color. In the past, I had been turned down on jobs because of color, but I never let it stand in my way. My Christian background helped me get through any situation. I believed that when one door closed in my face, God would always open another. I believed that with all my heart. Andy's problem was different.

After I started to work at the restaurant, I went and talked to my pastor about my job and the people that worked there. It was hard to explain to the Reverend everything that went on in their lives, but he got the picture. He told me to read the Bible, especially Romans. I began to read the Bible and other books about homosexuals. I could not find anywhere in the Bible where God approved of homosexuals.

I told Andy I was going to go to my pastor, so he was anxious to know what the pastor told me. The next day at work, Andy came to me and asked me if I had a chance to talk to the preacher. I told him yes, and I kept walking towards the kitchen. He ran behind me. He said tell him, but I didn't want to hurt his feelings. We were very good friends, and I knew I had to tell him the truth, but I wasn't ready. I told him

I would sit down and have lunch with him. He said okay, and he went back into the dining room area.

In my mind, I knew that God condemned homosexuals and all sinners, but I had a hard time telling Andy. I thought to myself, "I should tell him. If he knew the truth, would he change and become normal? Will he hate me and think that I am against him?"

I was confused myself. I knew that my problem was different from Andy's. My problem was about color. His problem was about sex, and God made us both. I didn't believe that God would make someone and condemn them afterwards. In Romans, it says that "Man should not sleep with another man, and a woman should not sleep with another woman." That's what the Bible says.

At lunchtime Andy joined me at the table, with a big smile on his face. What I had to tell him was going to wipe that smile off his face forever. Just as soon as he sat down, he asked in a very cocky way, "Well, Mama, what did that old preacher say?"

"He said you are going to hell," I replied.

He looked at me and began to laugh and laugh. Then I began to laugh, and we both were laughing. I didn't know why I was laughing though.

Soon he calmed down and leaned in closer. "That old preacher better be careful. He might go to hell with me."

He started to laugh again. I joined him so that we both laughed it off. I didn't talk to him about his sexuality anymore. I just accepted him as a person, and I didn't judge him. He was a person—a real life human being—and I accepted that. He never asked me what the preacher said any more.

My daughter, Debra, is a missionary teacher. She is a true Christian. At the time she was married and lived across town. I had not told her about Andy and the others. She knew I worked at Lathan's Café, but she didn't know the circumstances. She knew that I told her the place was weird, but she didn't know just how weird. She had worked at Lathan's Café on Gessner but not Richmond. This restaurant was different. Once you worked on Richmond, you would never forget.

I called her the night before, and we talked, and talked.

"Oh, yes, how is your job?" she asked.

"My job is fine. It's the people there that I would like for you to come and meet."

She laughed. "Why would you want me to meet them?"

"Maybe you can help get them saved."

Right away, she said, "Oh no, not me! Take them to church with you—let the preacher help save them. Oh no. No, not me."

"That's a great idea," I told her I will invite Sherry, Andy, Juan, and Pete to go to church with me Sunday. Meanwhile come have lunch with me tomorrow."

She said, "Okay."

We continued to talk for a while. It was getting late, so we hung up the phone and went to bed.

I was lying in bed plotting how I was going to set the scene for Debra when she came by for lunch. Somehow, someway I was going to get her to talk to the kids. Debra knew the Bible well; she could remember everything that she read scripture by scripture. I admired how she could talk for hours about the Bible. She was long winded just like a preacher. I had to plot a way to get her to talk to the kids at lunchtime, so, I carefully planned everything.

The next day I told Andy that Debra would be coming by.

"Ain't that the old missionary teacher?" he asked.

"Yes," I said with a smile.

"Why is she coming here—to tell us we are going to hell?" Then, he started to walk like Marilyn Monroe, in very slow-motion walking half sideways, looking over one shoulder with both hands on his hips. He stopped and started to rub up and down on one hip, and asked, "That mean old Devil going to stick a pitch fork in my hot buns, Mama?"

I was standing with my mouth open. I had never seen Andy perform like that before. I was shocked. I heard he worked as a female impersonator on Halloween. He acted just like a woman and could walk like Marilyn Monroe. Andy surprised me. I never saw this side of him. All I saw was a twenty-five-year-old young man, very well-groomed, waiting tables, and very polite to everyone. At that moment, I was looking at a Marilyn Monroe-type person who was doing a good job acting like a lady.

That day was the beginning of a new Lathan's Café. At lunchtime every day we had a show after we served lunch. At 2 p.m., we locked the doors, and the show began. Andy, Juan, and Pete would bring their drag clothes and put them in the storage room, until after lunch. Then they would get dressed like women, with makeup, high heel shoes, and the full nine yards. The manager would watch and laugh with the bus boys, the dishwasher, and the other waiters and waitress.

It was like I was growing up. Mama never let us go anyplace but school, church, and town on Saturdays. We never saw town until Saturdays, never a night club. Now, here I was in the restaurant where there was a bar with plenty of liquor. I had never seen a gay person, but now I work side by side with gay men and women every day. I had to pinch myself. I thought it was a dream and that I would wake up and none of this really was happening. But it was not a dream, it was real. These were real life people, and I was not like them, but they accepted me to be Mama.

The dancing began with loud music. The three guys would dance around the tables as we looked on. Andy was the leader. He was wild, and so was Pete. Pete was very muscular. He lifted weights, and his muscles sat up high and hard all over his body. Andy would act like the woman, very feminine. I never could figure Juan out. I didn't know how to describe Juan. He wore thick, thick eyeglasses with his hair hanging over them. He wore contact lens at the same time. His hair was cut short in the back and around his ears, but he wore it long in front to hang over his eyeglasses. I never understood him. He wasn't feminine or muscular. He was just ugly. He was always super nice to me. I loved all the kids at the restaurant, but Andy was my favorite.

The dancing continued for two hours. They would stand on the tables and dance. Andy had the long train of feathers that he and Juan wore around their necks, and they would throw it around another guy's neck and pull him up to them really close. They had fun as we watched. Juan was a belly dancer with bells all over his short costume. They didn't wear anything over their hips. They left the hips showing—just a slip between the hip. The hip had to show, as they would pass each other and grab each other's hips.

Jerry hired a new dishwasher, Melvin. He was a Black boy. He was straight—at least that's what the gay guys said. If you're not gay, you were straight.

This particular day after lunch the new dishwasher decided to attend the show. Melvin was sitting down eating, minding his own business when Andy decided to throw his feathers at Melvin. That was the wrong thing to do. Melvin jumped up from the table, threw open a switch blade knife, and swung at Andy. Andy was fast, and dived under the table. Melvin was after him calling him all kinds of names. Everybody was screaming.

I called loud to Melvin, and he looked around at me gritting his teeth so hard that I could see his jawbone moving back and forth. "He didn't mean it! He didn't mean it!" I yelled in a scary voice. "He plays too much. He didn't mean nothing." He stared at me for a long time, and I stared at him. He closed his knife and walked out.

Meanwhile, Andy was still under the table peeping out. When he came out from under the table, he started to cry from embarrassment because he didn't stand up to Melvin and ran under the table. "That's all right," I told him. "He probably would have hurt you. You have got to stop playing with everybody."

"This is the first time this ever happened to me. I am scared," he confessed.

"It's all right. He won't hurt you. I will talk to Melvin."

I was the kitchen manager. I could fire Melvin if I had to. I had a conversation with Melvin and I told him that I would not tolerate fighting on the job.

During our conversation, Melvin said, "Keep those punks away from me, and everything will be all right. I am not a punk pusher. I like women, not punks."

I told Andy, and we never had that problem again. In fact, lunches got quiet for a while. That action shook up everybody because someone could have gotten killed.

The next day everyone was laughing about what happened. In fact, they played the whole scene over. One guy played Melvin. Another guy played Andy who was running with one hand in the air and the other hand covering up his behind, saying, "Don't stick me. Oh, don't stick meme. Oh please, don't stick me with your big knife," and laughing. They had been sniffing cocaine the night before, so now they had nerves. They thought everything is funny. Andy said when he was high, he was Marilyn Monroe. He felt ten feet tall, so no one could touch him.

"Cocaine will kill you one day. You should change your lifestyle. You're young and talented, you are intelligent. I asked him, "Why do this to yourself?"

"I am trying to find myself. I don't know who I am. Don't you understand? I don't know who I am." He began to cry. He fell on his knees with both hands to his face and wept and wept. I walked away; I knew I would cry too. I wanted to help but I didn't know how. Their problems were deep down inside. Their pain was more than anyone could bear. They were in bondage, but only Jesus Christ could free them.

"You need to give your life to Christ," I said to Andy. "Let Him have control of your life. He can free you up, only Christ." He didn't want to hear that. He walked away.

I invited Andy, Sherry, Juan and Pete to my home. I also invited Debra. We had a fish fry because they loved fish. After dinner, I asked Debra about different scriptures in the Bible. She started to talk about love and that the greatest love is Jesus and how He loves everybody, and His will is that no man shall perish. They got really quiet when Debra was talking.

She went on to say, "But Satan wants you to perish. He pretends he is your friend. He is a great pretender. He makes you believe that taking cocaine is good, and he gives you a false high. He makes you think that you feel good for a while, but it does not last long because you have to do it all over again. It is a false high, but when you accept Jesus Christ into your life, you stay high on the Holy Spirit, and it won't cost you anything."

They listened, but I don't think it soaked in. They were really quiet and mellow.

When Debra finished talking, she left and went home. No one said a word about what Debra said. They were lying on the floor, so I turned the TV on and began to watch it. They stayed until the movie was over. Then they left. I knew they had to leave to go get high. They could not get high or drink at my home. I love them very much, but I had rules in my home. That was my castle.

The next day Andy asked, "Where is the preacher Debra?" He began to laugh and laugh. I could see he was laughing to cover up pain he felt inside. He knew that he was looking for everything Debra told him He was looking for true love.

He was looking for a good feeling—peace, joy, and happiness. Only Jesus Christ could give him that. Satan gave him false joy and peace for a while in drugs and liquor. When was gone, he had to start all over again, drinking and doing drugs to get happy. What Debra said haunted him. He tried not to let it bother him, but it was in his mind. He knew it was true. He asked me if he could talk to Debra again.

"Yes," I nodded. "Anytime."

He told me, "No one ever told me to shout Jesus. I would like to know more about Him."

I knew Andy was not as happy as he pretended to be. He carried himself like he was a happy person who didn't have a care in the world. His great smile was a cover up for the pain that he had in his life. He knew at a very young age something was wrong with him, and he didn't understand why he preferred dolls rather than a ball or toy trucks. He told me at the age of ten, a little girl at school kissed him on the cheek, and he hated her for that. He tried to wash it off, but he felt that the kiss was still there.

"I didn't understand why that bothered me so much," he explained. "I liked to kiss little boys but not little girls. My mother had always fussed at me because I would go into my sister's room and put on lipstick. I felt like my parents hated me. My mother would slap me in the face and wash my lipstick off."

As I listened to Andy talk, I wondered what was he thinking. Did he really feel that this was normal for a boy? I really wished I knew. It bothered me. I just wanted to think

Andy was normal and not gay. I really loved Andy; he was a true friend to me. He wanted me to be a part of his life; he included me in every event that went on. He wanted me to be a part of everything, but I couldn't be at everything I wanted to. I had to get my rest. I wasn't as young as Andy and the other kids. They could work all day and go out into the streets every night. I could tell when they would stay up all night because they looked like hell the next morning. I called Andy a vampire because he prowled the streets all night.

He would always laugh and never got angry with me. Sometimes he made me angry when he would play with the vegetables. He would put cucumbers into his pants and have the gay guys laughing. Sometimes he would put the cucumbers into his mouth and let his tongue flutter real fast at the end of the cucumber. He would laugh, and say, "Mama don't like me to play with the nice juicy cucumbers."

I would get angry with him, and I would tell him he was sick. He didn't like for me to get angry with him, but he loved to play. I would be busy, and he would play too much.

Sometimes I wore wigs to work. I liked wigs, especially when the weather was cold. But Andy didn't like for me to wear wigs.

I was behind the grill during lunch one day. The grills were full of steaks, chicken, and hamburgers. I was busy turning steaks and trying not to burn the marinated chicken. Because of the pineapple juice that we marinated the chicken in, the chicken could burn easily. All of a sudden, Andy came behind the grill, pulled my wig off my head, and ran into the dining area with it on his head. I couldn't stop cooking. But I was so mad at Andy that I could have set HIM on the hot grill. My hair wasn't combed; I was so embarrassed that I hollered and told Andy I was going to kill him. He paid me no attention. He was having fun with my wig. All the kids were laughing. I was smoking more than the grill was. I was so mad at Andy. When lunchtime was over, I cut off the grill, but Andy had left and gone home. I was glad because I believe I would have hurt him badly. He knew I was angry, so he called me on the phone and apologized to me. He really pleaded for his life. "Mama, I know I was wrong. Please don't be angry with me. I won't ever do that again."

"The only way I will forgive you is that you will have to work early and do my work—make salad, cut up chickens, and make salad dressing." He agreed.

For a week Andy came to work at 8 a.m., made salad, cut up chickens, and made salad dressing, so I forgave him. He constantly said, "I will do anything; just don't be angry with me. You are the only friend I have." I felt sorry for him and forgave him. He was an overgrown kid, so my heart went out to him. I knew he was not happy with his life. I wished I had a cure for him, but I didn't.

He had a limited education; he didn't finish school. He started to work at the age of sixteen. He tried to play football in school because his dad wanted him to be a football player, but Andy hated football although he liked the football boys. He said they were strong and very well built. He liked to take showers with the guys and watch their buns. He knew he was gay. After he couldn't make the football team, he tried to play basketball. He said he hated basketball, but this was a way he could be with the boys, especially when they showered. He said sometimes his parents would come to his games, but they would leave before the game was over because Andy would stay on the ground, or he would climb on someone's back. He embarrassed them so much that he just stopped playing.

He was disgusted with himself. He finally quit school and got a job at a flower shop. He was very talented in areas other than football. He said everywhere he'd worked he would become attracted to the boss man. He was 18 years old when he first dated another man. That's when he started going from town to town with different men. No matter where he went, he would write his mom and dad. He loved to send his mother birthday cards and money for Christmas, but she never answered him back or ever said thanks.

Andy had lots of pain. He felt nobody cared for him. At Lathan's Café we were a family, and Andy loved working there. I tried to be his friend and his mom. Andy felt he was just one of the kids at the restaurant with big problems. Little did he know, they all had problems.

I remember Rudy had been working at the restaurant for two months. He was a very weird person. He wanted to change the restaurant, but the restaurant chain had a policy of serving the same food in all the restaurants. They had a menu book that we had to cook from. We, all the managers and cooks, would meet once a month at a large hotel and learn of a new item that would be added to the menu book. This was a rule, and no one could change it.

Rudy wanted to change the menu. Rudy was Cajun and stood 5'5. He brought Cajun music to the restaurant. He would cook *Beans and Rice* and serve it for lunch. The supervisor didn't know it. He was really breaking the rules. I tried to warn Rudy. I told him if he wanted to serve something new, he should tell the supervisor, or else he was going to get into trouble. Rudy ignored me. He continued serving *Beans and Rice* and playing Cajun music. He was doing what he wanted to do. Although he attended the meetings and heard the president's warning to "never change the menu," Rudy still cooked *Beans and Rice*. The customers would eat it and enjoy it. Rudy even stopped serving the *Skillet of Beef* and started serving *Beans and Rice*. The supervisor would call him and say he was coming to the store, and Rudy would pull the *Beans and Rice* from the steam table and changed the menu back to how it was supposed to be. When the supervisor left, Rudy would change everything back. He got away with everything for the time being.

Every manager wanted the bonus money at any cost. Most of the time it costed them their jobs. I was just the kitchen manager. I did what the restaurant manager said, so I wasn't liable for what they did. The customers started asking for *Beans and Rice* when they would go to other Lathan's Cafés. The waiters and waitresses would say, "We don't serve *Beans and Rice* at Lathan's Cafés."

The customers would say, "Well, we ate *Beans and Rice* at Richmond and Shepherd." The word got around that we served *Beans and Rice*. The supervisors got wind of it, and the rest is history. We were getting a new manager. I saw Rudy cleaning out the office and taking his things to his car. I knew he had been fired, just like John.

The supervisor said that the restaurant wouldn't last because of all the gay people that worked there. We were out to prove him wrong. The restaurant could not discriminate against gays, so they hired anyone with experience. Our lunches began to get bigger and bigger. We were making lots of money for the restaurant. It seemed like everyone was happy, but there were lots of pain in the kids' lives. The shows they performed every day were a coverup for their pain. They really felt like rejects. The Army didn't want them. The police force didn't want them. Rejection hurts, so they pretended to be happy—but I knew better. I listened to the kids' problems every day.

One night, Pete was walking with his lover down the Montrose area, when a car pulled up. Several guys and jumped out and began to beat Pete in the head with a baseball bat. His lover ran and got away, but Pete was not so lucky. He was killed on the spot. I repeatedly warned the kids about walking down Montrose. On the corner at the end of the street was Lathan's Café. Before this happened, I didn't know that we were working in such a dangerous neighborhood. After Pete was killed by the gang, everyone was afraid to walk alone in the Montrose area especially the gay boys. For some reason society felt that gays shouldn't have been on the streets. We all went to court. The boys who beat up Pete were caught and convicted by law. We were glad that justice was served. Everyone has rights. Nobody has the right to kill because of a dislike for someone else.

I worried about Andy and Sheryl because they would get drunk and walk the Montrose streets at night. I prayed they would change. I couldn't understand why they wouldn't just keep it to themselves. Why tell others who did not know? Maybe they would accept them. I didn't know what to say or do when they told me how they were being treated.

AIDS FOUNDATION

wanted to help, so I decided to start an AIDS foundation. I loved the kids very much and treated them like they were my own kids.

I wrote to Austin, Texas to get all the information I could about AIDS. I went to city hall and talked to the mayor about starting a foundation, so I could help the kids. I wanted to do what I could. I didn't just want to feel sorry for the kids; I wanted to help. The mayor told me to get a charter and a form 501 (c) (3), and I could start an AIDS foundation. She said I could get funded if I had a 501 (c) (3), which would make my foundation exempt from taxes.

I began transmitting information via fax to different organizations to see who would help me with my foundation. I met a lady at the post office named Clara Johnson. I explained how I was trying to start a foundation. She was a very soft-spoken woman. When she spoke of her concern for people with AIDS, she stood about six feet tall, very large in stature. She wore a long wig. Her voice was so mellow that I thought she was telling me the truth when she said she was a CPA. A certified public accountant was exactly what I needed to get a proposal drawn up for my foundation. She was friendly and charming. I thought she would help me get my AIDS foundation started. I was so happy to know that. Clara called me, and we met at Lathan's Café after lunch to set up plans for the foundation.

I started to tell her my plans for the Helping Hands Foundation. I wanted an educational plan to teach people about HIV, the virus that leads to AIDS. I wanted apartments to house People with AIDS (PWA). She agreed and said I could get funding to help people. She left the restaurant. She was so happy, and so was I.

The next day Clara called me. She said she was sick and had no money for the doctor. She said she was anemic, and the medicine was gone. I told her to come by the restaurant and get $50.00 for the doctor, so she came and picked up the money. The following week, she called and told me that her husband wanted to work with us. He wanted to help get the foundation started.

I thought that was so nice of them to want to help me. She started calling me every day, and we would talk about the good things we could do for our community. I thought she was a nice lady. Three weeks went by, I was working, so I didn't have much time to spend on the foundation. But Clara and her husband did. She called me in the middle of the night. She said she needed money. Her house note was behind, and she was waiting on a check for her husband who had been hurt in a car accident. I felt so sorry for her. She was crying. I told her not to cry and that I would help her. I told her to come by my house early the next morning. I had money she could borrow, so she could pay her house payment. She and her husband came by the house and picked up the money to pay their house note. As they left, she said she would call me later. I didn't hear from her for a week. When she did call, she said, "I have some good news for you. We have an office building donated to the Helping Hands Foundation."

I was so happy! I would be able to help people get food, clothes, and pay some of their medical bills. I was so grateful.

"I will give you the address, so you can come and see the office building," she said. I will have a small brunch and invite some important people to come. Maybe they will give us a big donation."

After that, we got busy. Clara rented a word processor. She put in a water cooler, and she had full use of the telephone. The man that donated the building let us use the phone; we just had to pay the phone bill. I thought, "This is nice. Everything is going good."

A week later, we had a brunch at the new office. Clara had donuts, coffee, and fruit. She had everything set so pretty. As you walked in the front door over to the left, she had a nice table set up. She was such a professional and good at what she did. Clara had two teenaged daughters. They helped her with everything. She trained them well. They never said a word; they just did what she said.

I wasn't aware that Clara had received donations from people for the foundation. She never told me. In fact, she told me that she had no money. I believed her because she spoke so softly. Clara started to call places that she knew would give her money for the foundation. Grocery stores would give her food in Helping Hands Foundation's name, but she kept it all her for herself.

A week later, Clara called me at the restaurant and told me she had lost her car, and she had no transportation. I told her not to worry. She could use my car to get back and forth. I would have done anything to get the foundation started. The next morning Clara sent a friend by the restaurant to pick up my car. I didn't mind. I wanted her to help me. She called me at home that night and said, "I have good news for you. The mayor is going to help with the foundation, so we are going to have a cocktail party at the Ramada Inn, and invite the mayor. My husband Calvin will have a budget ready to present to the mayor at the cocktail party."

I said, "Oh great! That will be nice."

"I have a list of people with money who will help with the foundation," she said.

I thought to myself, "This woman was sent by God." I wanted to be able to help anyone with HIV or AIDS. My mind was on helping the kids and everyone else I could help. I was so happy.

On the day of the party, I arrived late. I was coming from Lathan's Café. When I arrived, I didn't see anyone but Clara, her husband, and their three children. They were huge children too. They were big and tall, just like Clara and her husband. The boy, who was 16, stood about 6'6 and weighed probably 300 pounds. The two girls were huge too.

I asked Clara, "Where is everybody? Where's the mayor?"

She looked at me with a big smile and said real softly, "They will be here. They called and told me so."

I tried to relax, but it was getting late. The cocktail party was scheduled from 4 p.m. until 8 p.m. It was 8:30 now, and no one was there. I was getting nervous. I didn't see that Clara and her kids were eating up all the food. I had given Clara $500.00 for the food and room. She said, "Don't worry; we will be able to give you your money back after the party." I didn't care. Whatever it took to get the foundation, I was ready to do it. I gave Clara money, and I gave her my car, so she wouldn't lose her home. I really believed in Clara.

Time was passing. It was 9 p.m. and no mayor or anyone else—just Clara, her husband, and their overgrown kids. By this time the food was gone. The kitchen brought out more food, and the kids were all over the table as though they never ate at all. At about 10 p.m. the manager said we would have to leave or pay more money. In fact, the manager brought a bill for the food. I told him to give it to Clara; she had paid up front. The manager said, "No, no—she did not pay. She said she was going to pay today." I looked around for Clara, but she had left the room. I was so angry. I had given her $500.00 out of my bank account to pay for everything.

She said, "Calm down," in a very soft voice.

I was breathing so hard. I couldn't calm down. I asked, "Why haven't you paid for the hotel?"

Clara said, "Well, I had to have a new dress, and Calvin wanted a tuxedo for tonight. Don't worry, I will handle it. Calm down."

I sat down, and I began to think. "What was happening? Was this woman for real? I had spent thousands of dollars and still didn't have anything for the foundation. What was happening?" I didn't want to accuse her and be wrong, so I relaxed and went back to the hotel. Clara's kids had cleaned out the food. They ate $500.00 worth of food—all of it. I began to get sick to my stomach, watching them eat. I was beginning to hate myself.

I wanted to stop right then and call it quits. I had had enough of this woman. It felt like a wheel spinning out of control but not moving. I was spending money and accomplishing nothing. I wondered whether or not she lied about the "people" and the mayor calling her? I had lots of questions in my mind but no answers. We cleaned the hotel room and left. I was puzzled about this woman and her family.

I went home and took a warm bath to relax my mind. But I could not get relaxed. I wanted to meet the mayor and the other people Clara had said were coming. That was why I had given her the money for the food that she, her husband and kids ate up completely. Why would she lie to me? She said she wanted to help me get the foundation started. I had no answers.

I didn't actually know who this lady was. I just had her business card that read "Clara Johnson, CPA" and gave her phone number. No address. I kept reading her card and wondered why there was no address. I finally fell asleep.

The next day, I called Clara at the office that she said had been donated to the foundation. She said, "I am so glad you called. The mayor would like to meet you."

I don't know why, but I got so excited. I wanted the mayor to know what I was trying to do for my community. I asked when and she said Thursday evening and that we would meet at the Palm Center Community Center, a new place. I got it for the evening without charge.

I said, "WOW! That's great, Clara! I'll meet you there Thursday evening."

I couldn't wait to meet the mayor. I wanted to tell her the problems that we were having in our community with drugs and AIDS. I wanted to tell her we needed more educational programs and more police protection in Southeast Houston. I wanted to tell her about the kids at Lathan's Café and how they couldn't get help at the hospital. I had a lot to tell the mayor, so I had a long list of things discuss.

Finally, Thursday arrived, and I made it to the community center. I was so excited when I got inside. I looked for Clara to find out what room we would be meeting in. I saw people standing in the entrance hall. I saw Clara's huge children and her husband, Calvin. I saw people from the radio station, all in the entrance hall. I finally saw Clara and asked, "What room are we in?"

"We couldn't get a room, so we have to use the entrance hall."

"Entrance hall?" I exclaimed. "You mean we are meeting with the mayor out here in the entrance?"

She had no expression on her face when she said, "The mayor couldn't come. She had to go out of town, so she sent Mr. Woods. He will represent the mayor."

I was shocked, but I held my peace. I went back inside. I just had to see how Clara was going to pull this off.

Calvin got everyone's attention when he announced, "The mayor couldn't be here, so Mr. Woods will present the proclamation to the Helping Hands Foundation."

I was just standing, waiting for Calvin to call me up to receive the proclamation, when Mr. Wood turned to Calvin and gave it to him. They never called my name; it was as though I wasn't there. I felt so hurt inside. They were trying to take my foundation. I was sick. I couldn't believe this was happening to me. Mr. Woods presented the proclamation to Calvin, while everyone stood watching. And I was just a guest, because they never called my name.

I left before it was over. I was so angry. Clara had said this would be my chance to meet the mayor. But Calvin was the director of the foundation now. That left me out. I was nothing. They could have introduced me to Mr. Woods or something, but they acted like I wasn't even present.

When I got home, I told my daughter Debra what had happened. She said "What? You better stop them. They are trying to take over your foundation. You better do some background checks on these people. They're just not right."

The next morning Debra called her friend Pat and told her what happened. She couldn't believe what had happened. Calvin was now telling everyone he was the director of the foundation when he wasn't. He was supposed to be a licensed CPA, but he wasn't. Neither was Clara. Debra's friend knew the couple because she was a CPA herself. That's why she knew Clara and Calvin. Pat told my daughter that Clara and Calvin worked as a team. They were very smart with IBMs and computers, and they could con anyone. And she said, tell your mother to get away from those people. They are no good.

When Debra told me, everything began to make sense. The cocktail parties where she'd said she had RSVP from— that was a lie. She had lied about needing money for the doctor. She lied to me over and over, and I had fallen for it each time. I only wanted to start a foundation to help people, while Clara and Calvin saw big buyers. The proposal was made for Calvin to get $50,000 a year, which was his salary plus the furniture, telephones, and buildings. The badge was big. I knew Mr. Smith with the AIDS Association. I acquainted him with Clara and Calvin Johnson. He investigated them and found out they were frauds. He called and told me that they weren't CPAs but professional con artists. I had to sit down; it was too much to take.

I got on the phone and called Clara. She acted as if nothing had happened. She was so calm and soft spoken. When I told her, I didn't want to do business she said, "I know. I told Calvin we should have given the proclamation to you."

"That's not the point," I explained. "You and your husband aren't CPAs. Mr. Smith investigated you two, and you are wanted for three counts of fraud and one theft of a car."

She never even got excited. "I'll call you tomorrow. It's getting late." She said before hanging up.

I couldn't believe she didn't deny anything. She acted like I had said nothing. I couldn't wait until morning. I called her bright and early. I told her I didn't want her to work for the foundation anymore. And I told her that Mr. Smith was not going to fund the foundation because she and her husband had ruined everything for the foundation. I said, "I don't ever want to see you again." And I hung up the phone in her face.

She called back in tears. I told her to dry up her tears because I wasn't buying that bull anymore and to bring back my car. I wanted it in one hour, or I was calling the police. She never said a word. In an hour, she was at my house with my car. She was crying and said she never meant to hurt me or the foundation. I told her to leave my house and never come back. I was hoping I'd never see her again.

The foundation had a small bank account of about $500.00 that we'd opened with donations from board members hoping we could do some fundraising to build the account. I didn't know that Clara had found the bank book in my car when she used my car. The bank started calling me, telling me that my account with the foundation was overdrawn. I said, "There must be some mistake. I never wrote any checks on that account."

The president said, "You'd better come to the bank, and get it straight."

I took the next day off from Lathan's Café and went to the bank. They showed me about ten checks that had my signature on them payable to Calvin Johnson. I never gave Calvin a check in my life. I didn't even like him. We checked the signature, and it wasn't mine. Clara had forged my name on ten checks. I couldn't believe this was happening. I went to the police station to file a forgery report on Clara Johnson. Her file was so long the paper folded over and over. I only wanted to help people, and now I was a victim of Clara Johnson. She had conned me out of all my money, as well as the money from the foundation.

During this time, the landlord where we housed the Helping Hand's Foundation called to let me know that his phone bill was over $600.00. Clara had made long distance calls to Calvin's parents in New York telling them he was the director of the Helping Hands AIDS Foundation. The landlord wanted me to pay for what Clara had done. I began to cry. This was too much for me. I was innocent. I was only trying to start a foundation to help people, and now I owed the hotel, the bank, and the landlord for calls Clara had made.

On top of all of that, she had broken my car I'd let her use. I couldn't understand why this woman wasn't in prison. She was wanted in three counties. Why wasn't she in prison? I had to go to all the places where Clara had written checks. It seemed that the store had let her write checks without showing identification, but I couldn't understand why the bank let her write a check at the bank and cash it without showing ID.

A week later, Clara and Calvin had planned to start working for Missing Children Foundation. They had found another person who didn't know them. Unexpectedly, Calvin had a fatal heart attack. I was sorry that Calvin died, but somebody had to stop them. Apparently, God did.

Clara called me crying about her husband, I told her to never call me again. I wasn't falling for her sad stories anymore. She had used me up. I wasn't going to let her get next to me ever again. She kept saying, "I'm going to pay your money back. I owe you, and I'll pay you back." But she never did. She moved to another part of town.

One day Mr. Smith called me and told me that a lady named Ms. Cartha wanted to meet me because Clara had conned her out of thousands of dollars, and she wanted some information from me, so she could put Clara away for good.

I met with Mrs. Cartha and another person whom Clara conned out of money. We met at a restaurant for lunch. We talked about Clara. I found out she'd conned about a hundred people that Mrs. Cartha knew. I was sick that I'd let her con me too, but after listening to Mrs. Cartha, I didn't feel so bad. She'd conned doctors, lawyers, and schoolteachers. She was a professional con artist. I felt so bad that I'd have to tell the kids at Lathan's that I wouldn't be able to start a foundation because of this woman. She really messed up a lot of lives and people that could have been helped through my foundation. I could have educated a lot of people in my neighborhood who so desperately needed to be educated about AIDS. People were so scared by AIDS because they were not informed as to how AIDS was contracted. Most Black people won't read, so for lack of knowledge they are getting AIDS and spreading it to their children and unborn babies. Oh, what a shame, and there was nothing I could do to help.

But this woman, Clara, had no guilt. She didn't care about anyone but herself, and the system couldn't keep her in jail. Mrs. Cartha called me and told me the police picked Clara up from the bank, where she was trying to put her name on an old lady's account. She would find old people and pretend to help them if their houses were falling apart or they had no food. She would call the city and tell the council when these people needed help. The city would go to the homes and take the media newsmen and newswomen, so it could be on the news. Then the public would see it and send donations. Clara was smart. She would choose a bank and put the address and phone number on TV where people could send or bring donations. Everything looked like it was all for the older people, while Clara was keeping the food and money for herself.

Mrs. Cartha was keeping tabs on Clara. Every move Clara made Cartha was watching. Cartha followed Clara to the Nations Bank along with Channel 26 and waited until Clara went inside the bank. Cartha followed her inside undetected. Clara went to the bank to meet with the president of the bank. Cartha had already called the president and told him about Clara. When Clara went into the office, they asked her what they could do to help her. She said, "I want to put my name on Mrs. Johnson's account. I have power of attorney." The president told Clara to have a seat, and he would be with her shortly. Clara waited and waited. The president sent a cab to pick up Mrs. Johnson.

While Clara was waiting, Mrs. Johnson walked into the bank. The president asked Clara again if she had the power of attorney over Mrs. Johnson's account, and Clara said in a very soft voice, "Yes, I do." Then Mrs. Johnson walked into the office. Clara did not get excited, but she tried to leave the bank. The camera men were in the bank too. They were all over Clara, asking her questions like why was she trying to get her name on Mrs. Johnson's account. Clara never said a word, but kept walking to her new Cadillac—the Cadillac in which the dealership was looking for.

That evening at 6 p.m., I saw Clara on "City Under Siege," a television show where drug addicts, rapists, and murderers were shown. There was Clara with no expression on her face, very calm when she told the newsman, "No one will help the older people, so I am only trying to help." I couldn't believe this woman. She was still ripping off people while the system allowed it to happen. Why couldn't she stay in prison? She'd walk in the front door and out of the back door. Cartha called me and asked if I had seen Clara on TV.

"Yes," I said. "Why can't they keep her in jail?"

Two weeks later, Clara went into hiding. She had packed up and left her apartment. Mrs. Cartha didn't know where she was. We were glad. We thought she had left town. Two weeks after that, Cartha called me saying she knew where Clara was. Cartha had to go to jail for a check she had written after Clara had paid her with worthless checks for some GET car phones, which made Cartha's checks no good. But the police picked up Cartha, not Clara. Clara got away clean again.

Cartha was a very attractive looking woman with a fair complexion, very short, curly hair, and very professional looking. I couldn't believe Clara had conned her, but if she did, she didn't have a moment's rest. Cartha kept her on the run.

Clara moved into a $250,000 home in Fort Bend County and wrote a hot check for $3,000 to move in. Cartha heard about it and called the realtor in Fort Bend to find out it was true, and it was. Then Cartha called the realty company and talked to Mrs. Chinn, a Chinese lady who had never heard of Clara. Cartha filled her in on Clara. Mrs. Chinn was shocked to learn the news about Clara. Cartha said, "I have a list of people who Clara has used false social security cards and drivers' licenses that do not belong to her. She is a professional. She is working with her two daughters since her husband died." Mrs. Chinn told Cartha to meet her at her office and bring the papers that she had, so she could have copies of it to get rid of Clara, but it was too late. She'd moved in during the night.

The next day, when Clara came to the office, Mrs. Chinn told Clara that she could not have the house. Clara never got excited when she said, "I moved in last night."

Mrs. Chinn said, "What did you say? You moved in? You can't move in. I do not sell my house to you, fraud lady. I have paper for proof, fraud lady. You used a wrong social security number. I tore up your contract."

Clara kept calm as she up and left the office. She went to her attorney to file bankruptcy, so that would give her time to locate somewhere else to live. Now they would have to go to court to get Clara out of the house that she never intended to pay for. She needed to stay in that house to keep her overgrown daughters in school, because in the black schools, everyone knew their mother. She was in and out of jail and always on "City Under Siege," a criminal TV show.

Meanwhile, Cartha had chased Clara for ten years, trying to get something on her, so she could go to prison. Cartha had ulcers, loss of appetite and sleep trying to track down Clara. Cartha called me from the hospital saying that she had ulcers, and her digestive system was messed up from a lack of rest and food. While she was in her hospital bed, she had informers calling her about Clara. She heard that Mrs. Chinn had managed to get Clara out of her house, and Clara was staying in a hotel with her overgrown daughters. Cartha told me where Clara was hiding in the hotel. I called Clara, and Clara never acted surprised when she said, "Who gave you my room number?"

"Cartha," I answered. I asked when she was going to pay me back the money she owed. She said, she'd have some money later that evening. She had pick up a check from a client, and she would call me back if I left my telephone number. I gave her my number, but she never called. She moved out that day.

Cartha was having surgery for ulcers caused from worrying with Clara. I lost money and my foundation, and Clara was still conning people. The system did not work. This woman caused an old lady to have a heart attack because she took all her money. She told Mrs. Hughes that she was investing her money, so she would never have to worry about money again because she would receive a check each month. Mrs. Hughes trusted her and gave her all her money. Clara and her overgrown daughters ate up all of Mrs. Hughes' money. Mrs. Hughes lost her home and became homeless.

THE NEW MANAGERS

Every three months we would get a new manager in training, who would train at the Richmond store. Then we'd get a new one, and the old one would go on to a larger store if the regional manager felt the person was qualified. Sometimes certain ones didn't make it.

After working with them for three months, I knew the ones that would go on to bigger and greater things. I knew Stan wouldn't make it; he was a new manager. He was gay and loved to party. He spent most of his time on the phone talking to his friends. He was a good manager, as far as keeping the food stocked. He would keep inventory every day, but after work he'd disappear.

I asked Andy one day, "Why does Stanley have to leave early every day?"

Andy said, "He has to get home to his lover."

"Lover?"

"Yes, Stanley is gay. Didn't you know that?"

"I heard he was, but I didn't know for sure."

Andy told me that Stanley partied every night at Numbers, a club on Westheimer. He said, "I want you to go with me sometime, and I'll show you the real Stanley. You won't believe your eyes. He's a different person when he leaves this restaurant. Wednesday night, I want you to make plans to go with man, and I'll show you what I mean."

That Wednesday night, we went to Numbers. I'd never been in a club that big. I understood why it was called Numbers. It was filled from wall to wall with people. You had to squeeze through the crowd, and it was so tight that when you did, your buttons came open. No one paid attention to us while we squeezed past. It seemed like we'd never get to the bar, where Stanley was.

Andy held my hand tight as he dragged me through the crowd. There were no tables or chairs, just people. I never saw so many people—all of them men. I felt out of place, but I wanted to know how gays lived. I was learning more and more about them.

We finally reached the bar. Across the bar drinking a large colorful drink with a tiny umbrella sticking out of it, was Stanley.

I said, "Stanley, that sure is a pretty drink."

He smiled but was shocked to see me even if he was too high to care. He just started dancing in one spot. He was wearing cutoff blue jeans, and they were cut high enough for me to see his buns. His lover started to dance with him, and he held Stanley's buns in his hands. When I looked around, everyone was dancing like that.

Andy asked me, "Mama, have you ever seen this many people in one place dancing before?"

"Never," I admitted "I've been to places where you dance, but the floor only held so many people at one time."

Since there were no tables or chairs to stop you, you could dance all over the floor in this place. I stood for such a long time that I couldn't stand any longer, so Andy and I left. He carried me home. That was an experience of my life. On my way home, Andy and I talked about the gay lifestyle.

He said, "Mama, you're a nice lady. Most people act like they're afraid of us, but you treat us like we're people. Although you don't approve of our lifestyle, you don't put us down, I love you for that."

"I'm not your judge," I said. "You're human, and I treat people like I want to be treated. God will judge us all. Jesus said for us to love each other as He has loved us."

After working with gays for so many years, I could see that all they really wanted was to be loved by their parents and by society, but they were rejected by everyone. I tried to give them love and support, but one person's love wasn't enough.

I REMEMBER JOHN, THE MANAGER

thought about how corrupt the restaurant was. If only I could change the people. The guys would be guys, and the girls would be girls. They wouldn't be confused. But I knew that would take a miracle to happen.

The managers were immature. They were young, fresh out of training, and vulnerable to everything. They needed lots of training. They were good with figures but not with people. They didn't know how to separate their lives from the restaurant, so their everyday living went on at the restaurant, including all their personal and restaurant problems. And I was in the middle of it all.

I never took sides, with the kids or the managers. Each one had a logical explanation, I thought. I tried to stay clear of any of the problems, but I didn't. I was always in the middle, trying to explain to the best of my ability. For some reason, they believed what I told them. That worked out fine. Each day there was a different problem. John was a Spanish manager in training from Mexico. He had worked at Lathan's Café in Mexico and gotten transferred to Richmond. I thought he was a nice guy because he pinched pennies for the restaurant, even though the supervisor didn't want him to. I found out that if the manager could save money for the restaurant, the manager could keep it for a bonus. The restaurant had a set budget for the month to spend. Managers who didn't spend it all could keep it. I began to understand why John wouldn't buy all the supplies we put on the list.

We needed brooms and more forceps and tongs to turn the steaks, but John said we had to wait until next month to get them. I didn't understand until one day I heard John talking on the phone saying how big of a bonus he was getting, and why and how he was getting it.

The next day, I made a big list for John, but he didn't order anything on it. In fact, he asked me if I could hold out another week and said he'd get me anything at that time. I asked why I had to wait. He explained, but I didn't want to wait.

Then the bartender came in and said her cream was sour, and she needed more to make drinks. To my amazement, John said to use it anyway. I looked at John knowing that the supervisor wouldn't like that because this decision could ruin the restaurant's image. The supervisor felt that we should never use anything two days in a row but to always make fresh salad, fresh skillet of beef, bread, and everything. But John would make us use things all over again the next day in his effort to save and get the money himself.

Well, the bartender called the supervisor to tell him about the cream and how John made us use it the next day when he knew it was sour. The supervisor was angry, but he didn't call John. He sent a decoy to the restaurant. The decoy came for lunch and ordered a Kahlua with cream. Kathy had to make it with the sour cream, and it curdled in the drink. The decoy asked to speak with the manager because it was curdled.

Finally, John came to the bar, and he asked, "What's wrong?" in a husky voice.

"My Kahlua and cream is curdled. And I want my money back."

"We can fix you another," John said. "Or you can have your money back."

"Well, then fix me another. This time I don't want to see it curdled." John had to find some cream that wasn't sour. When he couldn't, he asked Kathy why she hadn't told him the cream was sour. Kathy told him she already had, but he said to use it anyway. John got mad at Kathy because she was showing him up in front of the customer, who John didn't know was just a decoy for the supervisor. The decoy then said, "I was told you serve sour cream." He let John know that he was a manager from another Lathan's on the Gulf Freeway. John was in shock. He started to plea with the manager by saying it would never happen again. The decoy told him that if it happened again, John would be replaced. Then the decoy left.

John called the milk man and ordered new cream, but he got careless again and used the salad dressing and greens over again. He was supposed to make new salad every day, but he wanted to save money for a big bonus. Two weeks later, a couple came in when he'd used the same salad from the day before. The lettuce was a little brown around the edges, and the red cabbage was withered. It just wasn't fresh. John insisted we serve it.

I asked, "Shouldn't we make new salad?"

"No! I'm not throwing away perfectly good salad," he responded.

He should have listened to me because the couple had been sent by the supervisor without John knowing it. They were at the salad bar. When they got to the lettuce, the lady said, "This lettuce is brown." She wanted to see the manager. When John came out, he asked what was wrong, and the lady told him that the salad wasn't fresh. John, who was high on drugs at the time, was very rude and said, "If you don't like the food here, you can go somewhere else."

"Is that a fact?" she challenged him.

"Yes, that's a fact," he firmly replied.

The lady said, "Well, then let me call Carl, who sent me here to eat."

John's eyes bulged. He knew he was in big trouble. He tried to apologize, but it was too late. His job was on the line. He was sick. The couple put their plates down and began walking out. John ran behind them, pleading, but they never stopped; they left. John was just sick.

"Mama, I'm history, he said. I'll be fired. I know it!"

I felt sorry for John. I understood why he was trying to save money, but he needed to order what we needed. It turned out that other staff members had been calling the supervisor about John, and that's why decoys were sent.

The next day, Carl came himself and called John into the office. Carl told him the company needed loyal and trustworthy people to work for them, and they couldn't trust John anymore. John began to cry. It's hard to watch a man cry. He was hurt, but he was wrong. He should have done what the supervisor said.

MAMA AND THE LATHAN'S CAFÉ

"If something goes wrong, or if someone gets sick on this old food," Carl explained, "the president of the company will fire me. I stay on you, because the president stays on me."

They paid John for a month then fired him. This meant I'd be getting a new manager who probably had more problems, like all the others. I was tired of new managers. By the time I got used to one, he or she'd leave for another restaurant, or get fired.

I really hated to see John go. He was a good person, but he wanted to run the restaurant like he owned it. He had his own problems.

He told me once that he never touched his wife anymore. For nine years he hadn't touched her. They had a son born nine years ago, who'd drowned at the age of two in a swimming pool while his wife was drunk with her friends and not paying attention to the baby. John could never forgive her for that. She should have watched the baby. He cried bitterly when he told me about the baby boy, his only son. I tried to tell him that accidents happen and that his wife was being punished twice. Surely, she felt guilty about it, and he was blaming her. She had no support and would certainly crack soon. She felt bad enough without John treating her that way.

After I told him all of that, he said, "I can't help myself. I try to love her. I try hard." He sobbed and took a deep breath. He looked at me with red eyes and said, "I can't."

"But you have to," I insisted "She is going to crack up. She needs your support badly, but you won't help her."

I was thinking of this when I saw John crying in his office while Carl fired him. I thought, John needs support from his wife, but he never gave her any. What a shame. Now they needed each other very badly, and what a chance they were wasting because they hated each other. I knew he was hurting, but I didn't know what to say. All I could think about was how I could ever get involved in so many problems!

ABOUT BILLY

I t seemed as though anytime something happened, Billy, the morning manager, would always be on duty. Whenever someone decided to eat for free, Billy was always there. He was always on time, but he didn't seem to know what to do. For the first three months, he couldn't even boil water, which contradicted the prerequisite of being a manager. The manager was required to know everything pertaining to the restaurant's business. For instance, the manager had to know how to cook, wash dishes, bus tables, wait tables, clean up, and order supplies. Poor Billy didn't know much of anything.

One occasion six well-dressed men came into Lathan's Café during lunchtime. They appeared to be upscale businessmen because they ordered expensive items on the menu including steaks and the best wine. They seemed to be having a good time. After lunch, they got up, one by one, to go to the men's room and then quietly left the restaurant. Paula, the waitress at their station, noticed that the businessmen had left. She then whispered to Billy, "I think they're trying to leave without paying."

"Don't worry," he said. "I can handle them."

Billy began to watch them and noticed what was happening. The last two guys got up and proceeded to the men's room. Due to lunch being such a busy time for the restaurant, they proceeded to sneak out without Billy noticing. Paula, however, called his attention to it, and he ran outside to confront the men. The men, in return, physically assaulted Billy. The police were called and given the license plate number of the perpetrators. Poor Billy, he had only been at this restaurant about six weeks. Within this time, he had been beaten up and robbed twice.

It was just before Christmas, the busiest and happiest time of the year, when all was well with the business. We were booked for parties until the fifth of January and had ordered a sufficient amount of supplies so that we would not run out of anything. As we happily worked, we sang the prevalent Christmas Carol, "The Twelve Days of Christmas." We were so busy that we did not see two guys come in wearing masks and carrying guns. They got everyone's attention when they shot in the air. "Oh my God!" I thought. "I had never been in a robbery before." I began to pray. They then made everyone hit the floor with each person putting his or her hands over their own heads.

As I lie there on the floor, I began to wonder what they would do to us. "Will they kill us? It's Christmas." I began to think of everything and everyone dear to me. My kids—I wanted to see my kids. I then began to cry. I knew Billy had no money in the restaurant because it had been picked up the night before. He only had enough to open up with for that day, which was only fifty dollars.

I heard one of the robbers when he told Billy, "Give us the money; you know what we want."

"I have no money," Billy told them in a shaky voice. "They pick up the money at night. I have no money, just enough to open up with."

One of them said, "You are lying, you are telling a damn lie." He then hit Billy on the head with his gun.

Instead of knocking him out, they just made Billy mad. Billy was 6'6 and weighed 300 hundred pounds. He also played football in college, so he remembered being taught to tackle back when you get hit. Billy then grabbed the gun from the hand of the robber. Before he knew it, the robber began to run. Meanwhile, we were still lying on the floor.

The dishwasher, Melvin stuttered when he talked. He was so scared that we couldn't understand anything he said. Melvin tried to tell the police what had happened. He said, "I-I didn't kn-kn-know the-they was re-re-real rob-rob-robbers. Wh-when the-they t-t-told me to hi-hit th-that floor, I s-s-said Oh Shit!!"

The police were hysterical. They couldn't stop laughing at Melvin and Billy. They wrote their report with tears in their eyes. The whole robbery experience spoiled our Christmas spirit. We were sad for the remainder of the day. Instead of singing and being jolly, we began to think of what could have happened. The supervisor, Carl came to the restaurant and had a meeting with all the employees. He told us that during the holidays, robbers think that there's a lot of money flowing. As a result, they start robbing fast food restaurants.

Lathan's Café, however, was not a fast food restaurant. Most of the people that ate there were businesspeople who brought their secretaries or clients to lunch. They usually used credit cards as a means for paying for their meals. As a result, we didn't have a lot of cash like other fast food restaurants. Robbers didn't know this.

We wanted to be aware and look for anyone who looked suspicious. Billy put a plan into place. He said, "I want the back door with a lock on it and the back gate. Also, put a buzzer on the gate so that whoever wants to get in will have to ring the buzzer." Billy got busy and called a locksmith to install new locks. We felt secure. The gate and the back door were locked.

Two weeks later, four robbers came during lunchtime. The restaurant was full of people, and we were busy. They couldn't get through the back door, so they came in through the front door with their guns drawn. Everyone froze. Silverware was clicking as the people ate. Now it was quiet. No one said a word. Two of the robbers kept guns on the people in the dining room while two took Billy to the office which was in the back. They made him lie on the floor, as they proceeded to ask him questions about the money. "Where is the money?" one of the robbers asked.

"The armor truck just picked it up at one o'clock," Billy replied.

They had missed the money again. The robbers looked at each other with disgust and hit Billy across the head. This time Billy didn't move because two guns were pointing at him.

The robbers then went back up to the dining room. They were planning to rob the customers, but one man got up and tried to leave. They told him to sit down, but the man kept walking. Before we knew it, the robbers shot and killed him. They ran out of the restaurant. Everyone else was screaming,

"Call the ambulance, call the police, hurry, hurry, hurry!" But it was too late. Some of the customers tried to give him CPR, but they couldn't save the customer's life. When the ambulance arrived, he was dead.

The restaurant was not the same. Whenever we were in the dining area, we thought of the man that had gotten shot. Some of the customers got sick from looking at so much blood on the floor. This was such an awful experience that I wish I could have forgotten it, but I had so many memories.

EARNEST, THE BLACK DISHWASHER

I thought about Earnest. He was the dishwasher at night. Earnest was a short, 5'5—a real dumpy kind of guy. He often wore plaid pants with suspenders to hold them up. He also wore a wide leather belt that he said kept him from straining his back when he lifted weights. I could tell that he lifted weights because he was built. He had a very small waistline and broad shoulders. He was not bad looking, but he had a hard time keeping a girlfriend. I was curious, so I asked him how was his love life? He would smile and shake his head.

"Women don't like good men—they prefer a thing," he informed me You see, I am a good man." He then laughed.

He was a hard worker. He was also quiet and somewhat reserved. He would talk sometimes, but he mostly kept quiet. He liked to talk to me about his life, and his mother who he loved very much. He said, "I wish she was like you."

"In what way?" I asked.

"You aren't always putting people down. I don't care how bad the people are, you seem to look hard to find the good in them." He paused and then said, "I like that about you. My mother puts me down. She says I'm not worth anything and that I'm just like my dad."

Earnest began to tell me about the time he asked his mother why she married his dad. His mother got mad at him and went off. He said, "My mom and dad had been divorced for five years. My mother had been living with different men, and when I told her that I didn't like them, she wanted to put me out. Sometimes, I think that's why I can't keep a girlfriend. I think about my mom, and I don't want a relationship with anyone."

Although Earnest was very macho in stature, he was very sensitive. I saw him fighting back his tears when he talked about his mother. He really loved her, but he couldn't get close to her like he wanted. According to Earnest, she gave most of her attention to other men. I could see the pain Earnest was experiencing. I pretended not to see the big tear sliding down his cheek. I knew that would hurt him more. So, I changed the conversation and tried to joke with him. I asked him if I looked fat to him. He looked at me with a partial smile on his face and said, "No! No! You are not fat,"

I said, "Why are you lying? I am fat." He then fell on the floor laughing. I said, See I made you laugh." He walked away still laughing.

All the kids that worked at the restaurant really needed help—medical help!

Earnest had been peeping at the girls, when the girls changed their clothes in the bathroom. Paula spotted him twice, and she told the manager. However, they could not catch them. He would remove some of the ceiling. It was an Armstrong ceiling which consisted of removable small squared blocks. He would stand on the commode in the men's bathroom, remove the squares, and climb on top of the ceiling from the men's bathroom. It was beside the girls' bathroom, so he would peep when the girls used the bathroom or changed clothes.

The manager decided to figure out an intelligent way to catch Earnest. He put red invisible food coloring on the top ceiling. He set it up so that the "Peeping Tom" would get red food clothing on his clothing. The next day, the girls had finished dressing, and in walked Earnest with red food coloring all over his clothes. At the point, everyone knew that Earnest was the "Peeping Tom" or the "PEEPING EARNEST." The manager then called the police. They came and picked up Earnest. I really hated to see them handcuff Earnest and take him away, but what he had done was wrong. As he passed me, he dropped his head in shame.

THE MOUSE THAT WOULDN'T GO AWAY

I t was after lunch when all the stations were closed. It had been such a busy day. Everyone was quietly cleaning their areas. Andy was almost finished tallying his receipts for the day. Andy could always make you laugh no matter how tired you were. Andy began to share his experience about Ben, the restaurant's wood rat. Before you knew it, everyone had something to say about Ben. Ben would show up when you least expected it. All the waiters and waitresses knew Ben and had various encounters with him.

Ben was a big wood rat that lived in the restaurant for a long period of time. He was so huge from eating all the scraps and crumbs. Although Ben moved very slow, no one was able to catch him. His favorite time of the day seemed to have been during lunchtime. He often exposed himself during this time. We would all know when Ben was around. When we heard loud screams and trays crashing, we knew Ben was in the vicinity.

Ben was so smart that one day he visited the bar customers. During their good time, Ben jumped across the bar and onto the floor. It didn't take long for the bar customers to clear away from the bar.

Andy shared his experience about Ben. He said that one morning he had filled his tray with plates, baked potatoes, ice water, and bread and butter—only to have Ben run in front of him causing the tray to fall out of his hand. The tray, food, and Andy all hit the floor. We all roared in laughter.

Ben had been at the restaurant so long that I didn't think the manager was actually trying to get rid of him. When the manager, Billy, heard that the health department was inspecting all the stores, he put out traps with cheese to catch Ben. Needless to say, Ben ate the cheese without getting trapped. As a result, the "manager" called the city out to catch Ben. After closing at night, they put traps out all over the restaurant. Not only did they finally catch Ben, but they also caught his brothers and cousins. The restaurant was finally clean. No more Ben!

About two weeks later, I was in the kitchen marinating some chicken when I heard a loud scream.

I thought to myself, "Ben is back!"

"Wait, Ben can't be back," I mumbled. "We caught him."

I walked out front to see what was going on. A customer had a pet snake in her purse. She had left her purse open, and the snake had crawled out and into the waiting area. Everyone was screaming and running. The owner of the snake tried to calm everyone down. She said, "He won't bite you. He's a pet snake—a pet coral." She was on her knees trying to catch the snake. She tried to keep him from going into stations where other customers were eating. The waiters and waitresses were knocking over chairs, dropping trays, and running from the snake.

She caught him thirty minutes later. Our manager, Billy then asked her to leave. We thought Ben was a nuisance, but this snake made everyone clear the scene. Billy was very angry at the lady for bringing a snake to his restaurant. She could have run everyone away. He was so furious. He said, "I should have called the city to pick up the snake and put him to sleep or donate him to the zoo. I never should have let her leave with the snake. That's all we need is to be on TV, saying we have rats and snakes at the restaurant. We would have no customers at all." Billy then finally pounded his fist in his hand saying, "I wish she would lose control of her anal muscles."

Andy looked around and said, "Ooh" in a very snuggled manner. As he rubbed his hips up and down, he said, "That would be terrible, just awful, to lose control of your anal muscle." Everyone including the manager erupted into laughter. Andy could always make us laugh. He was a generous person with a good sense of humor. After what had happened during lunch, we really needed a good laugh.

ABOUT GEORGE AND KATHY

There were times we had to stand outside waiting for our manager George to open up. Now since I had the keys, we could get in on time and get things all set up before lunch. One morning, I got to work early because I had lots of work to do. I opened the door and ran all the way to the back to cut off the alarm. The alarm was already off. I thought that was strange. All sorts of thoughts ran through my mind. I thought, "Maybe a burglar is in here."

I went into the kitchen and looked around. I didn't see anything, so I assumed I was in the place alone. I started getting things together. That day I was to make a skillet of beef. That was our special. This particular recipe called for a little wine, so I went to the wine cellar to get some. The keys to the wine cellar were usually kept in a drawer by the refrigerator, but they were missing. I went to the wine cellar to see if somehow, we had forgotten them in the door. The door was ajar, and I started to think about the mystery burglar again. Tip toeing to the cracked door. I peeped in to see if I could see anything, and there was George on the floor making out with Andy. They didn't see me, and I ran into the kitchen as fast as I could and stood there in shock.

I was sick to my stomach, but I knew I had to pull myself together and try to get things ready for the lunch crowd. The doors opened at 11:15 am., and we had to be ready. George had to come into the kitchen to go to his office at the end of the room near the back room. It was close to 8:30, and he still had not opened the door so the dishwasher and busboys could come in. I kept talking to myself, telling myself I had to get out of this place. I knew this wasn't a place for amateurs. In fact, this place was not a restaurant; it was a nuthouse.

At 9 a.m. the secretary should have been in. I was hoping someone would come in. I was still a bit nervous and shaky. I heard the office door slam, and I felt relieved. I wasn't alone. I was so busy I didn't stop to see who came in.

Thirty minutes later I went to the office to tell the secretary what had happened with George and Andy. When I got to the office and opened the door, the assistant manager and Susie were smoking pot. His hand was inside her blouse squeezing her breast, and she was rubbing him between his legs. I shut the door, went into the kitchen, propped myself against the wall, and pinched myself to see if I was awake or asleep. I couldn't believe what was going on. I thought no one was going to believe me. This was a little "Peyton Place" and I had to get out. Everyone was crazy.

These people would all come in at 8:30 and 9:30 a.m. They were weird, but the people who came in at 11:00 a.m. were worse. Kathy decided to dress weird. I saw her punching her timecard, and I stood with my mouth wide open, staring at her. Her hair was sticking straight up all over her head, and it was streaked red, white and blue. She looked at me and in a soft voice said, "Hello, is something wrong?"

I shut my mouth, smiled, and said, "No, nothing is wrong."

She walked away. I slapped myself on the forehead and wondered what the people who ate here were like. I wondered if they came here to eat food or to satisfy their curiosity. I wanted to quit, but I really wanted to find out what everyone was like. As the morning passed, we hurried through lunch. Everyone was trying to serve as many tables as they could to make more money in tips. They cursed at each other, yelled, screamed, and did all they could to make more money in tips. They threw bread at each other and smeared whipped cream on each other's faces. The place was out of sight. I started yelling at them, telling them what I would not tolerate. I told them I was a Christian, so I didn't want them cursing around me. They stopped to listen. They started to act much better. I told them they should try to help each other and that they could all make more money if they cooperated.

It took some time, but they started to respect me and called me "Mama." They even began to trust me. They acted as though they needed and wanted someone to stop them and to treat them like someone cared for them. I found out that they were really seeking love. They began to talk to me more. Little by little I found out that they were very unhappy with themselves.

One day I was having lunch with Kathy, and she told me why she felt she was a lesbian and why she dated women instead of men. She was a very warmhearted person. I asked why she dressed the way she did; it seemed so wild and crazy. She said she didn't want to be attractive to men at all. She said, "I want a woman." She was dating a woman named Dean.

I told her she needed to find a nice boy and stop what she was doing. I said, "You're too attractive not to want a life for yourself. Maybe someday you might want a family of your own."

She stood up and shouted at me, "You don't know nothing! You must

have had a father and mother who loved you! I didn't; my father molested me ever since I can remember! Do you understand that?"

"I'm sorry," I whispered.

"Don't be sorry." Her voice seemed to elevate with each word. "My mother wasn't sorry. I told her what my father did, and she loved him more than me and put me in an orphanage. I was ten years old when a couple adopted me. My adoptive father did the exact same thing for six years. I was sixteen years old when I ran away from home. I hate men. That's why I'm a lesbian. I just hate men."

She started to cry. I cried with her and felt so sorry. I didn't know what to do. I kept wondering how I could help her. I went back to work, finished cleaning up, ordered for the next day, left, and went home. I had a family at home to cook for.

That night at dinner, we talked about the children's schoolwork, and they asked me what had happened on the job. I started to tell them what Kathy had told me, and they looked so sad. They began to feel sorry for her too. I started to cry again. My daughter thought she should see a doctor. I thought that was a very good idea and said I would tell her the next day. Before I went to bed that night, I said a prayer for Kathy—a special prayer that she would get her life together.

The next morning, the routine was the same. The manager was late as usual. I had to work extra hard to get the restaurant open to be ready for lunch by 11:15. After lunch was over, we all had lunch together in the Southeast room. It was a bit more private and larger than the other rooms, so we would have lots of fun together in that room. I couldn't wait to talk to Kathy.

We sat in the corner, and I told her about seeing a doctor to help her. She said she didn't have any money. "No problem," I said. We would find a way to see a doctor. I had to think of something to do. I told everybody to bring in their old clothes and anything they didn't want anymore. We were going to have a big garage sale. Everybody brought bags of old clothes, and I cooked barbecue and made sandwiches. That weekend I had a big sale, and we made over $200.00. I put the money in an envelope and gave it to Kathy. She was very grateful, and she hugged and thanked me. I was glad to do that for her.

After three months of seeing the doctor, Kathy was much better. I could see the changes in her. She cut her hair, and it was very pretty and naturally curly. It was dark brown instead of red, white, and blue. She began to feel really good about herself, and she would call me if she got depressed about anything. We sometimes talked for hours, and she would thank me for just listening.

Meanwhile, that night at dinner I told my daughter about Kathy and how the doctor had helped her, and Kathy was just thrilled about it. Ten months later, Kathy was really beginning to feel good about herself. She started to go to the spa and work out. She wasn't fat but thin, tall, and out of shape. She said working out helped her. A few days later while having lunch, she said, "Mama, I have some good news for you."

"What is it?" I said. "Tell me!"

We both started giggling. I felt good inside, seeing her laugh.

I met a guy!" she exclaimed.

There was an awkward silence. My mouth opened, but I couldn't say anything. I was so surprised. I just stared at her.

Then she repeated herself. "I met a guy! Can you believe it? I met a guy!"

I started to smile, and I asked her to tell me all about him.

"No, not yet," she declined. Not just yet."

"Okay," I said. "When you get ready to tell me, I'll be ready to listen."

"I keep thinking about the past," she confided. "But I want to think about the future."

"You will. It just takes time, but you will. Everything is going to be all right," I reassured. I told her she would meet lots of boys, and she would find the right one. When it happened, she should open up her heart and mind and give it all she had. "Put everything into it, and it will work for you," I advised. She thanked me. Lunch was over, and we went back to work so we could finish, clean up, and go home for the day.

On my way home, I kept thinking about Kathy. She was doing fine and was going to be okay. She really trusted me, and she was on her way to recovery. Thank God!

I rushed home to cook dinner for my kids and go to choir rehearsal. I had to sing Sunday morning. After rehearsal I got home about 10:30 p.m. and was getting ready for bed when the phone rang. I grabbed it, and it was Dean, Kathy's lesbian friend. She said, "I've got bad news. Kathy was coming home from work and stopped at the convenience store for sodas and cigarettes when two guys grabbed her and forced her into their car. They carried her to a wooded area, raped her, and beat her badly, then they dropped her into a parking lot. A maintenance man found her and called 911, and the ambulance carried her to the hospital. She's asking for you. Can you please come?" I said as soon as I was dressed, I'd be there. After finding out which hospital she was in, I rushed right over.

When I got to her room, she reached out for me and started to cry. "You just can't trust them." All of a sudden it seemed she was back where she was over a year ago.

"Don't worry, Kathy. We'll make it," I comforted her. "I'll help you, and we'll make it."

She held onto me and cried, "Don't leave me. Please don't leave me!" The nurse came in and gave her a sedative, and she fell asleep. I went home.

Every day I would visit. I thought she was doing fine. Sometimes I would notice that while she was talking, she'd find it hard to speak and would almost cry. I kept talking about what we were doing at the restaurant. I told her about Andy and Earl and how they would clown and what they'd done to Paula. Paula was a waitress that worked hard and fast. She would carry a tray of water glasses along with a tray full of food. She wore red underwear under her little costume. When she stooped over you could see them. Paula had her hands full on her way to serve customers when Andy sneaked up behind her and tucked her shirt into her panties. She was so busy trying to serve that she didn't notice what he had done. Everyone started to laugh, including the people she was serving. Andy was just cracking his sides. Paula asked what everyone was laughing about, and Janet told her she pulled her skirt out of her panties, and she began to laugh too.

Kathy thought this story was so funny that she sat up in bed and said, "Mama, how in the world do you put up with all of us? You're a good woman." For a moment she forgot all about her problems. Then the nurse came in and said that visiting hours were over, and it was time for me to go. I kissed Kathy on the forehead left and went home to get a good night's sleep.

Janet was on my doorstep when I got home. She was another fickle waitress at the restaurant. I couldn't figure her out. I didn't know what she wanted out of life. A tall, slender blonde, she liked to call herself Marilyn Monroe. She wore bright red lipstick, and her fingernails were bright red to match. She even tried to talk like Marilyn Monroe. She came to tell me that she was pregnant and didn't know what she was going to do.

"Who's the father?" I asked.

She said the baby was from Andy, who liked to call himself Alice.

I looked at her and said, "He's supposed to be gay."

"I know, she said. "I slept with him when his friend was out of town, so now what am I going to do?"

I wanted to know what she wanted from me. "I'm just a cook at a restaurant, I'm not a doctor," I commented.

She started to cry, and I said I would try to help if I could. Later on, I talked to Andy about the problem, and he said he would give her money to have an abortion. He asked me to tell her to leave him alone. She was always pulling on him and telling him she loved him. He'd tried to explain that he loved Robert, the guy with whom he had been living.

When Kathy got of the hospital, I invited her to stay with my family. She agreed. The day I picked her up, she wanted to stop by Chili's restaurant to eat. We sat and talked. She seemed to be relaxed, and I was happy for her. We had lunch and then went to my place. I fixed up our spare bedroom for her and put my television in there for her. She loved it. I could see that she was pleased with everything. She got into bed and immediately went to sleep.

The next morning, I went to work. Kathy didn't want me to go. She was afraid to stay alone. We had a long talk, and I finally convinced her that everything was going to be fine and that I would hurry back as soon as I could. "Call me if you feel depressed or afraid," I said.

She called me about six times. I was really too busy to talk, but I stopped to talk to her because I didn't want her to do anything foolish. I talked to her, and she would calm down. After staying with me and my family for about two weeks, she was ready to move into her own place. I told her that she had to be strong to survive. She told me that she was beginning to feel strong and felt she had a handle on things and went home to her own apartment.

She still called me every day. When she couldn't reach me, she would get hysterical. I tried to convince her that she should see the doctor again. She was starting to depend on me too much.

Kathy started seeing the doctor, and things started to get better, or so it seemed. It was time for my vacation, and I was ready for it. I left town on vacation for two weeks. Kathy just couldn't seem to handle that. She committed suicide. She had taken a bottle of sleeping pills and some cocaine. She left a note for me:

Dear Mama,

Thanks for all you tried to do for me. I can't stand it anymore. I'm not strong like you.
I love you very much.

Kathy

My daughter called me in Las Vegas, when I was getting ready to come home. I was sick inside. I had tried to help Kathy, but I couldn't. At the age of twenty, she was dead. I thought of her parents. What kind of people would do that to their own child? I became very angry with them.

I promised myself that I would not get involved with anymore of the people that I worked with. It was too much for me. It was worse than working in the hospital. The hospital depressed me enough, and this job was beginning to get to me too.

I REMEMBER JERRY, A MANAGER

Jerry had to leave overnight. He was transferred to Mexico where they opened a Lathan's Café. Jerry was the manager that hired me. I really did love Jerry. He was my manager and my friend.

He was married to a schoolteacher but was a womanizer. He was dating the bartender, Susie. She was very pretty, tall and slim with long blonde hair. Jerry fell in love with her, which was a NO NO! Company policy prohibited employee dating. Susie was pregnant from Jerry. We didn't know, but the supervisor found out and confronted Jerry. The supervisor told Jerry that he was aware of his love affair with Susie and the baby. He also told Jerry that if he wanted to keep working for the restaurant, he would have to leave town. Jerry was sick. He was very sad. He did not want to leave Susie, but he had to.

We sat and talked for an hour about it. He had to leave, or else his wife would find out, and he did not want that. Before he left town, he came by the restaurant to say his goodbye's. It was a sad day. Jerry was a true friend. He worked with employees, not just told them what to do. I was going to miss him very much.

The new manager had already started to work. His name was James, a very hyper German. I expected managers to be professional, but most of them were not. They were just common people. They were supposed to wear dinner jackets when in the dining room, but several of them didn't. Half the time they didn't even wear a necktie and were very unprofessional. I wondered how they got the job. They drank and smoked weed with the kids.

James was the worse one we had. He would come to work without shaving and holding his shoes in his hands. He would be late and had to finish getting dressed at work. I could have reported him to the supervisor. I don't know why, but I didn't. I didn't approve of his weed smoking. Although the kids smoked weed, they never did it on the job. James would drink and smoke on the job. James was hired to manage the restaurant. I wasn't supposed to, but I did. I would open up the restaurant in the morning and get set up for lunch. I would have to order the food or else we would run out. James knew I would take care of everything, so he didn't worry. My job was only to cook, yet I was the doctor, manager, cook, and a parent to my four kids on the job.

As time went by James got worse instead of better. His girlfriend was crazy. She would come to the store and act crazy. She would curse James out in front of everybody. One day Ann—that's James' girlfriend—busted in the store. She was angry with James. She cursed and threw cherry tomatoes at James. He couldn't stop her. They were wrestling in the kitchen. The whole staff watched, as she kicked him between his legs, and he went down. Then she fell on top of him crying, "I am sorry, I am sorry, I didn't mean to hurt you."

Then he got up and slapped her. She started to scream loud. The waiter and waitresses enjoyed every moment, but I was ready to quit my job. I had enough of everything. I put in my resignation. I wanted to be transferred to another store or resign. It didn't matter—I had had enough.

I called the supervisor, Carl, to talk to him about everything. He made an appointment to meet with me. He asked how soon did I want to meet. I said that same day, but he was too busy. He suggested the next day, and I agreed. I couldn't wait to meet with him. The next morning, we met at the restaurant. We sat down and had coffee. I started to tell him everything that had been going on for years. He didn't know—he really did not know about the hell I had been through with the kids and the managers. He was shocked to know all the things that went on in the restaurant. With both hands he stroked his hair back twice and stared at me. He really was surprised. He asked me if this went on in all Lathan's Cafés. I said I really don't know.

He looked at me and said, "You can't quit. This store would go under. No one would put up with what you have gone through." He said, "I am going to get you a raise. You deserve a raise; I had no idea all this was going on."

"No one made me put up with this," I shrugged my shoulders and said. "I thought I could make a difference. I thought I could help change lives. I really wanted to, but it's too much for me. I get involved with people because I care."

I told him that Jerry was the best manager we had, but he couldn't keep his hands off of the waitresses. Since Jerry left, things got out of hand. He told me things will be different.

"You'll see." Carl said firmly. "I am going to clean house if things don't change around here."

I was glad I talked to Carl. I felt better. I really didn't want to leave. I felt like the kids needed me. I knew that they needed someone. Their lives were so empty and meaningless—no goals in life—just living from one day to another. Things did get better. The supervisor had a staff meeting, laid his laws down, and it worked. James started to come to work on time, and he was fully dressed, with a necktie and a clean shave. I was impressed. I thought maybe this was a new beginning for everybody. This lasted for several months. Finally, James, had finished his training at the little restaurant, and he would be leaving for a larger restaurant. There were many Lathan's Cafés all over town, but this one was different, very different. James left to go to New Orleans.

MEMORIES OF PAM, THE DANCER

fter Lathan's Café closed for the day, I drove to a different restaurant. As I sat in my car, so many memories of the things that happened at the café came to mind (one thing after another). I began to reminisce about Pam. She was special. Pam was an Italian girl with very tanned skin. Her hair was coal black, and she wore a size three dress. Pam was very tiny, but she was also very strong. She had a strong mind in that she knew what she wanted, and she went for it. Her goal was to be a dancer. She could dance very well.

Pam said, "Nothing is to stop me. "I want to dance, and that is what I am going to do. My family thinks I'm nuts, but I want to go to New York and dance on Broadway and Carnegie Hall."

I listened as she sounded off and expressed the things she wanted to do. "I want my name up in lights someday."

I was proud of Pam. She was determined to become somebody. "I am not going to wait tables all of my life, and you will be proud of me—really proud, Mama," she said with a confident smile.

"I am glad you have a goal in life for which you are striving," I said. I am already proud of you.

Pam and I had a special bond and relationship. I guess I had special relationships with all the kids. Her parents told her dances don't make money, and she needed to go to school for something worthwhile. They said, "You're wasting your time dancing." But she loved to dance, and she was born to dance.

Pam went to dance class twice a week, and she began to get better and better. She would dance in the kitchen. She watched her weight, and she would work out in aerobics every day after work. When I worked in the kitchen, I would often run her out. She loved to dance. Sometimes, I would be too busy to watch her, but she danced anyway. Pam would dance by me and untie my apron. She would then run out of the kitchen laughing. She was very energetic and full of life.

We were getting ready to have our annual Christmas party at the Hilton. All of the employees were invited. I remember how pretty she looked at the Christmas party. Pam was dressed in a red and white dress along with a red and white cap on her head. She was beautiful, as usual. Pam spotted me through the crowd and came over to my table. She sat and talked for a while. She then began to dance. Everyone had begun to dance. Everyone asked her to dance because she danced well. We all danced and had fun. It was a beautiful party. I noticed how late it was at 1 a.m., so I decided to go home. I was extremely tired, and my feet were hurting from dancing. I had worked all day at the café, so I left the party and went home.

At approximately 3 a.m., I received a phone call from Andy. He called to tell me Pam had been in an accident on the way home. I asked Andy if she was alright, if she'd been hurt.

Andy stopped me and said, "Mama, just listen to me, please. Pam is dead. A drunk driver ran a red light and hit Pam's Volkswagen on the driver's side and threw her onto the street. She died at the scene."

I began to beat the wall. I was numb and speechless. I just wanted to run, scream, and never stop running. I had lost so many of my kids to AIDS, suicide, and now a car accident. How much more could I stand? I felt as though I was losing my mind. I had to get away. I just had to. I couldn't take anymore. It was too much.

I began to realize that I was farther than I wanted to be because I could feel their pain. This was the very reason I decided to stop working at the hospital. I had gotten too involved with my patients. It wasn't any different at the restaurant. I was too involved with the kids.

I had to take a vacation. I was trying to think so fast. I knew I couldn't leave the kids because I loved them too much. I was just fooling myself. I started to think about Pam and all of her dreams of becoming a dancer. I realized that her dream to dance on Broadway and Carnegie Hall would never be. She was eighteen years old, and her life was over because of some drunk driver. What a shame!

It began to get late, as I sat in my car reminiscing about the kids and the restaurant. I then decided to go home.

I REMEMBER DORIS

Doris was the clumsiest waitress I had ever met. Although she was very attractive, she was clumsy. The manager hired her, and she told him she needed work really badly. George thought he was going to date her. He didn't know she was a lesbian.

On her first day, she got dressed up in her short costume and looked like a waitress. She filled her tray with water glasses, bread, and butter. She didn't even make it to the dining room. She dropped everything on the way.

All the waiters and waitresses ran to help her; they cleaned up her mess and gave her another tray. This time the tray was full of food, steaks, and prime rib dinners. Doris made it to the table that time, but she hit the lady at the table on the side of the head with the tray.

She began to apologize to the lady who said, "That's okay, everything's all right."

Doris put down everybody's food and went to get the drinks for that table. She got the drinks, and while she was trying to serve the drinks, she dropped them all in the same lady's lap.

The lady got angry this time. She jumped up from the table and got all over Doris. She was wet all over. Doris tried to apologize, but the lady wouldn't accept it. She demanded to see the manager. Doris kept saying, "I'm sorry? I'm sorry!"

The woman kept answering, "You're right about that. Go away and stay away from my table! Just leave me alone!"

Doris began to cry. George came and gave the lady and her friends a free lunch. Doris was still crying. She said, "I quit, I can't be a waitress."

George didn't want her to quit. He was thinking of himself dating Doris. But he was mistaken; Doris liked women.

So, George offered her a position as a door host. All she had to do was seat the customers, but she still messed that up too.

Doris was dressed like a door host, but she couldn't even seat people properly. At lunchtime when the restaurant was rushed with people, Doris got confused. She was seating people at the same table instead of making sure the table was unoccupied. She was so confused that George had to come out of the office to where the waiters and waitresses were fussing over the tables. It was a mess. George, himself, had to finish seating the customers for the rest of the day, and Doris ran out crying and holding her head.

I felt sorry for her, but she just couldn't do the job right. When lunch was over, George asked Doris if she wanted to be a bartender. She said, "No, I never fixed drinks before."

Then George said, "Okay, so I'll have your check ready for you."

ROSY, THE DISHWASHER

We never knew who Rosy was. She came to the restaurant looking for a job. George, the manager at the time, was optimistic about hiring her. Rosy was a gypsy woman. She told George that she was desperate for a job. She said she lived under the bridge with other homeless people, and she wanted to get herself a job and find a nice place to live. She had no ID, and I think she made up her social security number. Yes, she was weird, but so was Lathan's Café, so she would fit in perfectly. George hired her.

She came to work dressed with two head scarves on her head, two coats, three pairs of pants, and some dirty, dirty tennis shoes. She smelled very bad. George told her she had to wear the required uniform—blue pants and white tee shirt, and she had to take a bath if she wanted a job. He gave her the uniform. She left and went home or wherever she lived.

George offered to take her home, but she said no. She didn't want anyone to know where she lived. George was curious. He said to us, "I'm going to follow her and see where she lives."

Rosy got on the bus, but she never got off. She just rode on and on. She slept while she rode, but she didn't get off. Finally, the driver woke her up and put her off the bus.

George had to stop following the bus after about three hours, so we never found out where she lived. The next day, Rosy had on her uniform, but it was on over her other clothes, and she still hadn't bathed. The manager told her he couldn't use her anymore, but she pretended she didn't understand.

Finally, he said, "I'll give you your pay from yesterday, and you don't have to come back."

"Okay," she said.

He paid her, but she kept on working. She was slow. Dishes piled up everywhere. She couldn't keep up with the dishes because she still wore her coats, head scarves, pants, and the uniform. She just couldn't move fast enough with all of those clothes piled onto her body. George tried to help her, but she wouldn't take a bath or get rid of all these clothes. She got upset when George told her she needed to take a bath and take off some of her clothes.

Rosy was weird, but George couldn't get rid of her. He fired her and hired a new kid named Perez, a Spanish boy. He was very fast. He had everything set up and ready to go when in walked Rosy. She told him she was the dishwasher. Perez was confused. George came in and told Rosy that she'd been fired and couldn't come back anymore. He had to be firm and even get hostile with her because she kept coming to work. He told her he'd call the police if she didn't leave. After several hours she left.

George opened the front door for lunch and went back to his office. When the dining room was filled with customers, Rosy was one of them. She sat in the dining room ordering lunch. She had come back as a customer. Her body odor was bothering other customers, and they asked to be moved to another room. That's when George came back. He was furious with Rosy. He asked her to leave, but she refused.

"I'm a customer, and I'd like a menu."

"You have to leave, Rosy. You're running off our customers."

She still refused. George went to the office and called the police, and they came and took Rosy away. They didn't take her to jail, just to the bus stop and told her never to go near Lathan's Café again. She agreed and said she wouldn't.

The next day she came again at lunchtime. She never sat down. She just walked in and used the restroom and left. She knew that would annoy George, and it did.

SHERYL, THE LADY MANAGER

Sheryl was a white female with long blonde hair and big blue eyes. Everyone liked her from the day she began working at Lathan's Café. Not only did she have a great personality, but she was also a very hard worker.

Sheryl rarely asked anyone to do anything that she could do herself. I thought to myself, "We finally have a manager who knows what to do for a restaurant." She basically monitored everything including the walk-in ice boxes and the storage rooms. Sheryl even took inventory because the other managers often stole steaks. Some were caught red-handed with a full case. Billy fired the dishwasher and two busboys because he thought that they were guilty. The assistant manager, Paul had been stealing steaks and selling them for drugs.

One night, Billy, the manager said he would be leaving early to go home. Paul gladly said, "I will close up for you tonight." Billy then pretended to leave but actually sat out by the garbage can in someone else's car. When Paul later took the garbage out, he was also taking one box of steaks to his car. Billy saw him and ran over to Paul. He told him, "Drop those steaks!" Paul began to run but Billy caught him and immediately fired him.

The following day, Sheryl came to Lathan's Café. She helped me make the skillet of beef, onion soup, and she even set up the salad bar. We had everything ready at 10:30 a.m. The other managers had never helped at all. They only took the credit for all of the work I did.

At 2:00 p.m., when the front door was locked, I wondered what Sheryl would say when she saw the freaks come in. We were sitting in the Fifties Room when Andy, Ike, Janet, and Paula came in, jumped, and danced from table to table. Sheryl loved it. I could tell by her eyes. I thought that she wouldn't like what was going on, but she just joined in. Sheryl had on tight jeans and high heel shoes. The fact that she jumped right in let me know she wouldn't last three months. After two weeks of working at Lathan's, she began to get just like the other managers. She would call in and say she was going to be late because she had partied all night with Andy and Ike. They were the gays. They were too neat, clean and always well-groomed.

Andy was the head waiter. He handled himself well. He made more money than anyone else. He was very fast. While all of this was going on, I was behind the grill. It was so hot that Buddy brought in a fan just so I'd be cooler. He was very nice to me, and we got along well. In fact, I got along with everyone. We were like one big family.

The first of October, I was in for a surprise. Everyone was getting ready for Halloween. Everyone was making costumes. During all the preparations, Buddy hired new waiters. Sheryl fell for one named James. He liked to call himself Jagloe. He was tall and thin, with curly hair. Sheryl thought he was cute, and soon afterwards they started to date. Every day she would tell me new stories about James.

Halloween finally arrived, and everyone was invited to a ball which was being held in the home of a physician. No one knew who the doctor was because it was a costume ball. I was also invited to the ball, and I was excited to see what was really going on. No one looked like himself. Andy was the queen of the ball. His costume was a silver jumpsuit with silver boots. He wore a silver beaded cap with a train that stood about a foot long and silver tassels hanging. To top this off, the mask he wore was silver with pearls. Of course, he won first prize.

To keep from being alone at the party, I asked my daughter and a friend to go with me. When we arrived at the doctor's home in River Oaks, I was impressed. It was enormous. The front door of the house was guarded by two marble lions. Each of these stood in front of tall white columns. We walked in, and no one even noticed we were there. The music was deafening, and everyone seemed to be in a daze.

Sheryl was there already. She was dressed in a costume from the Roaring 20's. There was one man dressed from head to toe in balloons. Every time he passed someone, one of his balloons would pop. Eventually he was stark naked, and he continued to walk around that way. It didn't seem as though anyone minded. They didn't care or just didn't notice. It was a weird party. There was plenty to eat, plenty to drink, and plenty to smoke.

My daughter and I walked around tasting the wonderful food, and no one even noticed. They were in a different world altogether.

Mark, who called himself Mary, walked over to us and started complaining about his feet. He was angry because his feet were so big. He or she wore a long, white silk dress and looked very nice. He also wore tennis shoes because he couldn't find size 12 white satin pumps. He just stood around and complained.

Shortly thereafter, we left this scene. No one noticed when we first walked in, and no one noticed when we left. In fact, no one really cared. I assumed Sheryl went home.

The day after Halloween, everything was quiet. Everyone was tired. Most of them didn't even go to bed. Andy and Ike still had on eye make-up. Monica, of course, was still complaining about his or her feet.

After two months, Sheryl started doing everything the gays did. She cut her hair very short and wore her jeans even tighter. In fact, she had to lie down in bed to zip them up. By now, she was so in love with James that she wanted to marry him. What she didn't know, however, was that he was bi-sexual. He liked both men and women. She didn't realize this until after they had been intimate. When Sheryl found out, she was devasted and asked me to join her at another restaurant. After clocking out, we went to Chili's. She ordered a Wild Turkey straight up. I said, "That bad, huh?"

She nodded her head. She started telling me how much she loved James and no one else. She then told me how much she wanted to marry him. Sheryl said, "Every time I try to tell him how I feel, he changes the subject to something else." James had taught her how to meditate. She worked so hard at it and was sure it really worked. She would often pretend to be in another town.

The next morning, Sheryl was crying. She had walked ten blocks to work because James had her car. She didn't even know where he was. I told her she knows where he was, and she began to cry again. I told her that she knew that he was with Pete.

I said, "He told you he wanted Pete, so you'd better get yourself together and leave James alone."

Her voice quivered when she said, "I can't."

I then walked away and continued to work. I knew that if I didn't, lunch would not be served at lunchtime.

Sheryl said, "Let's talk at lunch."

"If I have time, we will," I told her. I didn't want to talk to her because she had a "hard head," and I knew that she wouldn't listen to me.

At lunch, we sat together in the Fifties Room. It was very quiet. We started talking about James again.

I asked her, "Why don't you drop him for a while, and see what happens?" He didn't have any money, so she would always pay whenever they went out. Sheryl, however, didn't seem to care about that. She just wanted to be with him. Sometimes, she would even cash her check to take him out. Once, she cashed a check for $500, and they did cocaine together.

The next day, he came back to work and brought her the keys to her car without saying a word about where he had been in it—not a word. She just looked at me and walked away. She started to follow me and play with her ear. Usually, when she would play with her ear, she was either serious or lying.

"What's your problem now?" I asked.

She wanted to know what she should do. I felt as though she needed to think about it for a while.

Sheryl was scheduled to be off that weekend. She said that she would stay home, rest, and try to get her life back in order. During this time, Sheryl had a roommate named Mary. They had been best friends for quite some time. Mary went to Dallas for the weekend. Mary's boyfriend came over to find Sheryl depressed. Somehow, they managed to end up in bed and making love to each other. Afterwards, Sheryl felt guilty and called me to confess this. I was supposed to ease her guilt.

I was getting ready for Sunday worship services when she asked if she could attend my church with me. I told her that I would be glad to have her go with me. One hour later, she was in front of my house. I looked out through the curtains in the den, and she did not look well to me. I asked her what was wrong, and she began pulling on her earlobe again. She wanted to talk about it after church.

On the way to church, she said Pete would meet us there. I felt that church would help her. I said, "Reverend Roberts will be pleased to see you. I've told him so much about my white kids. I told him about my four Black kids and ten white ones." Throughout the church service, Sheryl and Pete were a bit nervous. They stared at each other a lot. Baptist churches are loud. Two hefty ladies kept jumping in the aisles. That made Pete more nervous than ever. He had never been in church. He said, "Never." I put my arms around him and told him to relax. Sheryl pretended to enjoy the service. The music started and they both loved it. The lead singer, Debra, sang like Aretha Franklin. She had a lovely voice. The singing was fine, but when the minister started to preach his sermon, I could see that they didn't care very much for it.

During various songs, Pete would tap his feet to the beat and rock from side to side. When the ladies started jumping in the aisles, he would squirm in his seat. They were glad when the services ended. Reverend Roberts asked all visitors to stand. Sheryl stood and said she enjoyed the service and hoped to come back. On the other hand, Pete was frightened. He refused to get out of his seat. Again, I placed my arm around him and told him to relax. "You don't have to stand up if you don't want to," I whispered. He was ready to go.

We left and went back to my house for Sunday dinner. Pete followed us in his car.

While we were at the table to each lunch, Pete was still shaking. When I asked what was wrong, he said, "Sheryl and I were the only white people in the building."

I just stared at him. He got up from the table to demonstrate what he is feeling.

"When I stood up, I could feel them shooting me in my back," he exclaimed. He was serious. Sheryl and I began to laugh. He looked at us, and then he started to laugh too. "No laughing," he said. He then said he had borrowed everything he wore because he didn't have any church the next Sunday. I was pleased to hear him say that. We ate, and they helped me clean up afterwards.

Later in the day, we took a nap. It seemed they were so relaxed at my home. It was quiet, and they could rest. I believed in going to church. It gave me strength. After hearing the problems of everyone on the job and trying to take care of my family, I was glad to go to church and fall on my knees and pray. It was the only thing that kept me sane. Without Jesus in my life, I didn't seem complete.

The next day at work, we had more trouble. There was always something happening at Lathan's Café. I kept a diary because there was always something new. Today, Sheryl was sitting in the walk-in ice box. She sat on a tomato box with her hands under her chin. I asked, "What's the matter?" Are you so hot you have to sit here?"

She looked up and said, "I told you I slept with Mary's boyfriend while she was in Dallas. Now she's mad with me. I'm so ashamed of myself. I don't know what made me do it. I don't know how I could have done such a horrible thing to my best friend. She's hurt and so am I." She started to cry again.

I hated to see people cry. I would cry with them. I was angry with Sheryl because I had talked to her about drugs and what she becomes when she takes them. She just didn't seem to care about anything. Now she wanted sympathy from me. I was crying, but I wanted to slap the hell out of her.

"Mary is moving out today. We have been roommates for five years, and now she's moving out." She cried harder.

"What do you expect her to do—live with someone she can't trust?" I asked softly. I did feel sorry for her and patted her on the back. "This too will pass," I reassured her. Revered Roberts always said, "When one has problems, he or she should just say, 'This too will pass.'"

Weeks passed, and Sheryl's spirits were lifted. She started going out with the gay boys. She was trying to forget what had happened with Mary. She said, she was having nightmares about it. She would dream Mary was trying to kill her. She felt Mary was watching her because she'd threatened to get even. I didn't volunteer anything. I just listened. I really didn't know what to say.

The next morning, Sheryl was late for work. When she finally arrived, she was angry and crying. At this point, I had to tell her, "You're the manager, not me. Why do you come to work? I'm tired of lying to the supervisor for you. You better do better, or I'm not going to cover for you anymore."

"I'm sorry, Mama," she apologized. "But somebody cut my tires on the front of my car," she sobbed. I think it was Mary. She hates me. I just can't live there anymore." She kept crying and insisted that Mary would kill her.

I told her to stop saying that. "Mary's not that kind of girl."

"Yes, she is. You just don't know her like I do. She used to buy guys tires and cut them up when they made her mad."

That weekend, Sheryl moved in with James and Pete. She still loved James, but she was also trying to get him out of her mind. It seems as though she had jumped from the frying pan into the fire. Sheryl wanted too much from James. She wanted to take him to bed every day, but he refused. He started making her listen to soft music, really soft music, to take her mind off sex. She wanted to marry him badly, so he slipped off and left her.

She didn't know that he was leaving town. He left, and he didn't even tell her goodbye. I thought she was going to kill herself. She was sick. She locked herself in her apartment and wouldn't come to work or even answer the telephone. I was finally able to get a key from the manager to get into the apartment. When I got inside, Sheryl was as white as a sheet.

I thought she was already dead. I picked her up and put her in the shower and put cold water on her.

She began to come to herself. We were all glad she wasn't dead. I told her, "The supervisor wants to talk to you." But she wouldn't talk to anyone but me. She said everybody was her enemy, and she didn't want to talk to anybody.

I brought Sheryl to my home, and she stayed there for two weeks. I cooked and got Sheryl to a big bar-b-que, hoping to reach her, but I never could. She just cried, and I did too. She was in love. She wouldn't work. She didn't want to do anything but sleep. So, I came to work every day and left her at home. I'd call back to see if she needed anything.

The supervisor came to the café to see if he could talk to me about Sheryl. He told me to tell her that when she got her life straightened out, to give him a call, and she could have her job back. She'd worked for Lathan's Café for seven years, and she'd always been faithful to her job. She couldn't handle being in love, so she left town.

She left town and didn't tell anyone anything. I called all over town and talked to all of her friends including Andy, Ike, Pete, and Janet. Nobody had seen her. Everyone seemed to think I knew where she was and wouldn't tell them. Two years later, Sheryl called me. I was so happy to hear from her. She began to cry. She finally went home to James. They went on a long vacation and made up with each other. They had a guitar shop and were happy. She still calls me and thanks me for making her get off drugs and get her life together.

ABOUT MARK, WHO CALLED HIMSELF MARY

Mark was the blonde that I saw in the restaurant the first day I applied for a job. Mark stood 6"6 and weighed about 140 pounds—very thin. He had long blonde hair that hung over his shoulders—his thin shoulders. He had beautiful hands with manicured fingernails—very well groomed.

Sometimes he would refer to himself as Mark; other times he would say that he was Mary. That part he was confused about, but one thing was for sure. He hated being a man. He hated everything about his body. He wore a size 13 shoe, so he hated his feet.

He asked me, "Why am I trapped in this man's body? I'm a woman! I like everything a woman likes. I can't be a man," he said banging his fist against the wall.

He hated himself, but he didn't have the money to get an operation. He didn't make enough waiting tables, so he was very depressed. He didn't know what to do with his life. When he would talk to me, I just listened. I didn't have an answer for Mary or Mark—whoever she or he was. He didn't know who he was, and I didn't know who he was. It was sad.

I watched him when he waited tables. He would lean over to take an order, and his long hair would hang across his face. The way he walked and talked looked like a woman, but he was a man.

I had worked in the hospital for fifteen years and never faced anything like this. I never thought I would, working at a restaurant. People had so many problems. Mark worked at the restaurant for two years, saving all of his money. He stopped buying clothes and eating normal. He ate only one meal a day, so he could save enough money for an operation. After two years, he finally made it. First, he had to see an endocrinologist who started him on hormones, twice a day. His chest began to grow like a lady's.

The endocrinologist told him, "Once you start this procedure, you can't turn back, so you'd better be sure."

Mark said he was sure. For two more years, Mark took hormone pills. He said he felt like a woman and that he would go through with the operation.

Six months later, Mark had the surgery. He was a woman. This was very confusing.

Now he said, "You can call me Mary. I no longer have a penis. I have a vagina." He appeared to be so happy.

He asked Billy, the manager if he could dress like a woman. Billy said he could, so he began to dress like a waitress, with the short plaid skirt and black tights. His breasts were sticking out; he had put silicone implants in them. He looked like a real woman. But I could tell he wasn't happy even though he pretended he was.

A month went by. One day the Carl, the supervisor came to the store. He stared at Mary. He thought he recognized

Mark, but wasn't sure. He went to the office and asked Billy if that was Mark dressed like a woman, waiting tables. Billy tried to explain that Mark had an operation and was no longer a boy, but Carl, didn't understand.

Carl said, "If you're born a boy, you are a boy. You are not a girl."

Billy could tell that Carl didn't like it. He tried to explain with greater detail, but Carl got more and more angry.

He started hollering at Billy. "How could you let this happen? How could you? I know that we have gays working here, but they wear pants, so no one knows. We can't have boys wearing girls' clothes and waiting on customers! That's not right. I won't have it!"

Billy was upset, Carl was upset. Carl went out front where Mary was waiting tables. He fired Mary on the spot. He told her to punch out and go home. Mary started to cry. She needed the job to finish paying for her operation and to pay her rent. She knew it would be hard to get another job. She had not quite gotten the hang of how to do things as a woman, and couldn't get a man's job. He was a woman now.

Mary was devasted. She left the job running. I tried to stop her, but she kept running. I felt so bad, but I knew Carl was right.

"This is not a freak show—this is a restaurant." He was cursing loudly. Everyone got really quiet. When he finished, he told Billy he'd get back with him.

Billy was so nervous. He asked me if I thought Carl was going to fire him. I didn't know.

"I don't think so; he's just angry," I said. Let him cool off, and then he'll make a good decision."

I was thinking to myself that Billy had messed up. He should never have let Mark dress like a girl and wait tables. I was worried about Billy's position.

Two weeks later, Carl came to the restaurant with the president of Lathan's Café. I knew Billy was in trouble. They called Billy into the office and closed the door. We tried to eavesdrop, but we couldn't hear anything. They stayed in there for about thirty minutes. It seemed like forever. We could hardly wait until they left.

As soon they were gone, we ran to the office to ask Billy what had happened. He said really sadly, "They fired me."

I said, "What?"

"Yes," he said. "The only reason they gave was that they can't use me in the company anymore." He looked at me and said very loudly, "I risked my life in this restaurant so many times." He began to scream.

I said, "Calm down, Billy, please."

He was hurt and kept screaming. He sat down at his desk and began to cry. We all were crying. Billy was a good manager. We all liked him very much and would miss him.

"They never gave me a chance to explain why," he said shaking his head. "I was trying to keep Mark, and I hurt myself."

He asked everyone to leave him by himself for a while, so we left him alone. He called his wife. The door was half open, I could hear him blaming himself. Then he said, "What am I going to do now?"

Three weeks later, Mary came by the restaurant. We had a new manager, Allen Jones.

Mary asked, "Where is Billy?"

"Billy got fired for letting you work the floor dressed like a girl," we told her

Mary was so hurt. She said, "No, no," and grabbed her face with both hands. She turned red in the face, screamed, and ran outside the restaurant.

I went behind her. That was the story of my life—running behind the kids when they were hurt or in pain. Mary was in the parking lot. Her face was so red. She felt like it was her fault.

Once she got calmed enough to speak, she said, "I just came here to talk to you about my operation."

"What about your operation?"

"I'm not happy with it; I want to reverse it."

"You want to be a man?"

"Yes." She paused and dropped her head. "But I know it's too late. The doctor told me I couldn't ever go back. I'm so mixed up. What am I going to do?" She began to cry in the parking lot.

People were coming and going, and they began to notice Mary crying.

I told her, "Let's go back inside, where people won't notice so much."

Mary agreed, and we walked back inside.

Mary told me everything. "I can't get satisfied being a woman," she whispered. "It's just not working. I don't want to have sex with my vagina. I want it anally like I did before." She kept crying while she talked.

I couldn't outright say I'd told her so, but I did mumble the reminder, "I did tell you to think twice before the operation."

She didn't catch that quick reminder. Instead, she said, "I'm sure it is what I want because this is just not working out." In that moment, it seemed like she processed what I mentioned a few minutes ago because she asked, "What do you say?"

I didn't know how to help Mary. I was at a loss for anything to say. I just offered her a glass of iced tea or coffee. She said, "No, thanks. I need something stronger."

I was afraid she'd kill herself. Oh, I didn't know what to do to help Mary. Finally, I thought of something. I said, "Mary, there's a Catholic Church that's open 24 hours a day on the corner of Alabama and Richmond. Go there and confess. Maybe the priests can help you. I know you can go there now and tell the priest everything. You'll feel much better."

She agreed and left. I was so worried about Mary. For five years she'd worked to save money for an operation that she was now unhappy with it. She had large silicone breasts, even.

"Oh, my God! How could Mary change back?" I kept wondering.

I couldn't handle work for thinking about Mary. I knew that something had to be done, or Mary would commit suicide. I just knew it. What could I do? My mind was racing. Poor Mary. When I got off work, I went straight home to call her. I got out of my car and ran to her door and knock with urgency. I had to talk to her. I banged on the door and waited for a few minutes. She wasn't at home.

After leaving, I went home and dialed her telephone number. The phone rang with no answer. It seemed like I became obsessed with needing to talk with Mary. I kept dialing and dialing, but no answer came. Finally, I got her on the phone very late. I asked her if she would have lunch with me Saturday. She said yes.

When we met for lunch, she looked very bad. She hadn't been sleeping at night. She had dark circles under her puffy, red eyes. Between not sleeping and the cocaine, Mary looked like hell. The waiter brought us two menus. Mary said, "I'm not hungry; I'll just have coffee."

I ordered, and while we sat and waited for the food to come, Mary began to cry. I asked, "What's wrong?"

Mary replied, "Everything, just everything."

"What's wrong now?" I asked.

She began to tell me her truth. Mary had gotten a letter from her mother, whom she hadn't heard from or seen in twelve years. The family had disowned her when they found out she was gay. Mary would write home and get no answers, but she kept writing. Mary found out her father had died. He had two daughters—real daughters—not homemade like Mary. The father wanted his son to carry on the business, and not the daughters. The father wanted the business to stay in the family name from generation to generation. But now Mary was a girl like her sisters. It was confusing. As she talked to me, we both started to cry. No one in Mary's family knew about the change. She asked, "How can I tell my mother and my sisters that I've changed?" By this time, she was devastated and hysterical.

I couldn't calm her down. I kept saying, "Think about it for a few days. You don't have to make a rash decision now. Give yourself time to think about it."

Mary began to calm down. Then she looked at me and said, "I might as well be dead. I will never get the millions my father wanted me to have because I'm a girl. He didn't want a girl to have the company. It's been the McCulland Trading Company for 40 years, so my father wanted the company name passed on to my son." Mary began to cry again. She was so sad. Now her eyes were even more swollen and red. She said, "Unless my mother feels sorry for me and gives me my inheritance, I will be on the street the rest of my life."

Now I understood why Mary wanted to commit suicide. I wanted to kill her myself. I didn't know that Mark had left a mansion back home, to become Mary because his family couldn't accept his homosexuality.

"Let me tell you something, sister!" I declared. "You have millions of dollars to collect, so you better find a way to collect. Do you understand? You need to stop feeling sorry for yourself, and let your brain start to work for you."

We began to put our heads together. We thought one thing after another. Some ideas sounded good, and some sounded so bad, we laughed.

Mary said, "I know what I'll do. I'll cut my hair and dress like a man. That's what I'll do. I'll go shopping and buy some more clothes." But she forgot about her big breasts. "Oh, God, what will I do with these breasts?" she asked. "I'll have to have surgery and have them removed."

"Good idea," I said You better get busy before they read the will."

The New Mark

Several months passed while Mark was trying hard to get his life together. He had surgery but wasn't healing. We didn't understand. Mark just wasn't healing properly even though removing the silicone wasn't a major surgery. In fact, it wasn't that big of a deal. Months went by, and Mark was still draining from the breasts. Mark got so disgusted that he cut his wrists with a razor blade and had to be rushed to the hospital. He was near death.

When I got the news, I went straight to the hospital where Mark was. I knew I had to get to him. His mind was messed up, and I would be the only person that he would listen to. I was very tired and sleepy, but I had to talk to Mark. He was in ICU, and only close relatives could see him.

I went to the nurse's station and was looking bad—I know. I didn't have time to change my clothes or fix my hair. I just rushed as fast as I could.

The nurse asked, "Who are you?"

"I'm his mother," I replied.

The whole staff froze for a second and looked at me as if I were crazy.

"I'm his mother," I repeated Let me in. I have to see Mark."

The nurse kept looking at me and reading the chart. She finally said, "Mark is white." Then looked up at me.

I said, "I know what you think, but I'm his mother. Please let me in. He has no other family but me. Please let me in."

The nurse was a very tall person, and she looked big. She said in a very gruff voice, "I will give you five minutes. That's all."

I thanked her and went in to see Mark. Tubes were everywhere. Mark was asleep, so I said in a low voice, "Hang in there, Mark."

He opened his eyes and looked up at me. He never said a word, but tears slowly fell from the side of his eyes. I didn't want him to see me cry, so I held my tears back. It was hard, but I didn't cry.

I slowly rubbed his forehand, kissed him on the forehead, and said again, "Hang in there, Mark. I will be back tomorrow."

I left and went home to get some sleep. I was so tired.

The next morning, I went to the hospital early. I knew I'd only be able to stay five or ten minutes, so I could get to work from the hospital. When I got to the hospital, I went into the nurses' station. This time I looked better. I was dressed; my hair was combed, and I smelled good. They let me in without any problems. When I saw Mark, they had removed the tubes from his nose and only had one IV going in. I knew that Mark was better.

When he saw me, he began to cry, "I can't do anything right. I can't even kill myself. I messed up again."

I said jokingly, "Why didn't you call me? I would have helped you kill yourself."

Mark laughed. I knew then he'd be alright. I left the hospital and went to work. At work I thought of Mark all day. I was trying to work out a solution, but I couldn't get anything to work right. I wanted Mark to come and stay at my house, so I could take care of him. I knew that my son would not approve of that. In fact, he had nothing to do with gays, so that wouldn't work. I had to think of something else.

I was really worried about Mark. I decided to ask Andy if Mark could stay at his apartment for a couple of weeks, until he got better.

He said, "Oh, yes. I don't mind, Mama. I'll do it for you."

I said, "Thanks, Andy, I knew you'd help me."

When I got off work at four, I rushed to the hospital to see Mark. They had moved him to a psychiatric ward for observation. I was glad. Mark needed help that I couldn't give him. They wouldn't let me see Mark. I couldn't go into the psychiatric ward—not even for five minutes. I begged, but they refused. The doctor told me it would be 24 hours before I could see him. I was very disappointed, but I understood. I left and went home. On my way home, I just rode around to get Mark off my mind, but I couldn't.

I drove through the River Oaks area. It was decorated so pretty. It was Christmas time. I drove from one street to another, looking at the lights. That relaxed my mind; I loved Christmas time anyway. It made me happy inside. This was good therapy for me to drive and see the decorations. I felt better after several hours, so I drove home.

The next day I went to work back at the restaurant, and my mind was relaxed. I knew that Mark would be all right, and I kept thinking that he would be home soon. During my break, I called the hospital to talk to him, but they told me that Mark had no phone in his room.

I said, "Well, take a message, and have him call me."

"No, Mark can't call you," the nurse informed me. "He can't leave the room."

I asked in an upset voice, "What is going on? What have you done to Mark? He was just supposed to be observed for 24 hours, then come home. What's happened? It's been 24 hours and more. Why can't I talk to or see Mark?"

The phone conversation was not good for me at this point. I hung up the phone, jumped into my car, and went to the hospital. I got to the nurses' station, but they grabbed me.

By this time, I was furious. I said, "Let me go! I have to see Mark. Let me go, and get your hands off me!"

The nurse said calmly yet firmly, "Calm down. Mark doesn't want to see anyone. He told us, 'Don't let anyone in to see me.' That's what he told us. So that's why you can't see him."

I started to holler and cry, "Let me see Mark. Let him tell me himself. I don't believe you."

The nurse was now losing her patience with me. She quite loudly, "Mark told the doctor everything about how he changed over from a man to woman and how unhappy he was living as a woman and how he lost his inheritance because he was a woman. He said he tried to fix things, but he doesn't feel he can. He keeps making a mess of his life. He said he kept hurting you, and he wants you to get out of his life, so you won't be hurt anymore."

The nurse kept talking, telling me what Mark had said, but it wasn't sinking in. I heard the words was saying. I just didn't want to be shut out of Mark's life.

I started opening the door to Mark's room, but the nurse stepped in front of me. She looked me in the eyes and said, "And Mark has AIDS, too. He doesn't want to hurt you. He loves you. You've been a mother to him."

"Can't you understand? I pled with her. "That's why I have to be by his side. I'm his mother. He has no one else, only me. Nobody understands him like me."

Then I broke down and I began to cry. The nurse hugged me and took me into her arms. I cried and cried. She took me to the nurses' lounge, brought me coffee, and tried to talk to me. I was hurt. I didn't care if Mark had AIDS. He was still my friend. I wanted to help him if I could. He needed somebody to talk to, and he could talk to me.

The nurse said, "Listen to me for a while. Yes, I know how you feel, but you need to go home to your own family. They need you too. Mark will never get well. There is no cure for AIDS. I'm sorry, but that's a fact. You should leave. There's nothing you can do."

I didn't want to, but I left and went home. I couldn't get Mark out of my mind. Days and weeks went by. I hadn't heard from Mark. Why wouldn't he call? I was thinking all sorts of things in my mind. I tried to think of good things but couldn't. I had been to the AIDS foundation. I know how AIDS patients look, how skinny they got, and the sores they got all over their bodies. I kept thinking, poor Mark. He tried to make a new life. Should I write Mark's mother and tell her about Mark? I didn't know what to do. I didn't want to do anything Mark wouldn't to do, though. I was all mixed up with my thoughts. So, I called Andy. I was hoping he could help me make a decision.

Andy told me to let go. He said, "Mama, please let go. You've done all you can do for Mark. These things happen, and there's nothing anyone can do but let go."

I tried to let go. I knew he was right, but it was hard to let go. I stopped calling and trying to talk to Mark. I just went to work and tried to get my own life together the best I could. I had lost so many of my kids to AIDS, suicide, and car wrecks. So much had happened at the restaurant, until I hated myself for ever working there. I thought it would be fun to work at the restaurant. I didn't know that the people there had so many problems. The reason I had stopped working at the hospital was because the people there had so many problems that I decided to find a new job. I thought working at the restaurant would have jolly times and laughter. I was very wrong. From the manager to the kids, they all had problems.

I would ask myself over and over, how did I get involved here? Why am I here? I had plenty of questions but no answers.

Two Months Later

Mark called me at work. He'd gotten out of the hospital. He was much better and rested up. He had been in counseling, and his mind was better. His illness turned out to be HIV, not AIDS.

It had been months, and I was glad to hear Mark's voice. He said, "I have got to talk to you."

My mind clicked. A light came on in my head reminding me not to get involved. "I'm going out of town this weekend, Mark. Maybe I can see you when I get back. I'll call you," I said before quickly hanging up.

I knew I wasn't going out of town. I just didn't want to get involved anymore. I was trying to pull myself away from the problems at the restaurant. I had finally started to feel better. I'd gotten some rest. My nerves were calm now, so I didn't want to get caught up with Mark anymore. After I hung up the phone, I felt good. I said to myself. I am not getting involved again, and I got busy doing my work.

Into the café walked Mark. He had cut his hair and gotten some men's clothes and shoes. I'd never seen Mark in men's shoes. He would wear sandals or thongs. Now he had on black men's shoes that tied. I was shocked.

He said, "My name is Mark McCelland. I'm not Mary anymore." I just listened when he talked. He said, "I'm sorry. I didn't want to talk to anyone in the hospital. I had to get my life together. I have had time to think, and now I'm going to be Mark. I'm going back home to see my family and tell them what I've been through. I'll tell my mom I have HIV and that I'm dying. I'd like to see my family before I die. I hope she'll accept me. I've been gone so long. I hope she understands like you. I was wrong. I know I've been wrong. I never should have left home. I never should have had surgery and changed my whole life. I've made so many mistakes. While I was in the hospital, therapy helped me see my mistakes. Mark admitted, "Whatever happens to me, I've only got myself to blame."

I was impressed with Mark. Although it was late, he had changed—I mean really changed. I looked at Mark, with his short haircut, neatly-trimmed fingernails, and he really looked like a man. For once in his life, he really knew what he wanted.

Then he said, "I'll be leaving tomorrow, but I had to see you before I left for New York."

When he reached out to shake my hand. I could see the cuts on his wrists, where he'd cut himself with the razor blade. I thought about how he'd tried to take his own life. But now that he wanted to live, he had HIV, and he was going to die. How sad I felt for him, but I hid it and didn't cry.

"Be sure to write me when you get to New York," I said keeping emotional distance. I just didn't want to get involved anymore. He walked towards the door, turned around, gazed at me, and waved. I waved back and said, "Don't forget to write, please."

Two weeks later, I got a letter from Mark that said,

Dear Mama,

When got to New York, my family was glad to see me. When told my mother that I had HIV, she told me that I couldn't stay with her and that I had to leave since my life and the way I lived was different. She said, 'Your dad wanted you to have the business, but when we never heard from you, I sold it. I do have some money for you in a trust fund, but you can't stay here. Why had you come back? Why didn't you just stay where you were?'

Mama, I was so hurt! I knew she wouldn't understand like you. She never tried to understand me and never listened to me. She just won't deal with problems. That's why I left home the first time. I thought it would work. I've changed, but my mother doesn't care. She doesn't want her high-class friends to know she has a gay son. So, I'm leaving.

I don't know where I'll be tomorrow. I'm leaving New York and going to California. I'll write you from California. I don't know if I'll ever see you again. But always remember, I love you, and you'll always be my mama.

Mark

I REMEMBER HURRICANE ALICIA

As I sat in my car looking at the restaurant. I couldn't help but to remember the storm.

The sun was shining bright when I got to work. I had not listened to the weather report. I didn't know we were in for a hurricane. Everyone began to arrive at work at their usual times. Andy made the coffee. He had to have a cup or two to get started because he was always hung over from the night before. Soon, everyone had arrived, and the radio paused for a news bulletin. We listened when the weatherman said, "There's a hurricane on the way to Galveston."

We all shouted together, "Galveston!!"

This means we'll get it next," the newsman said. He then advised, "You should tape up all windows and move to higher ground."

However, Billy, the manager said, "That storm won't reach us—maybe tomorrow. Everybody get back to work."

We began to prepare food and set up for lunch. The sun stopped shining, and the sky was really dark, we kept preparing for lunch.

I told Billy, "We better tape up the windows."

He said, "The storm probably won't even come this way. We might get some rain and a little wind. There is nothing to worry about." We listened to Billy and got ready for lunch.

Lunch began at 11 a.m. However, when we opened the front door, no one came. We should have left then, but we waited and waited. Still, no customers came.

I told Billy, "We better close and get home."

"Oh no, it's just raining," he insisted. We probably won't get the bad storm."

It was going on 2 p.m. when the wind blew harder, and the rain started to gush. It seemed as though someone was pouring it in from buckets. The wind blew the front windows away, and the rain came inside the restaurant. Billy hollered for us to get some plastic bags and try to close the windows, but no one moved. We ran into the liquor room and left Billy out front trying to sweep up the water in the front area. We didn't help him because he wouldn't listen when we tried to tell him the storm was coming.

Billy got soaking wet. His hair was washed over his eyes, and he could barely see. The wind was so strong. He couldn't even shut the door. We felt sorry for Billy and began to help him. We tried to put the food away, but we couldn't work fast enough. The water was too forceful. It knocked us to the floor.

I was scared. I didn't know what to do. I tried to help, but I was so scared. I had never been in a storm. I wanted to go home, but I couldn't. It was raining too hard. I thought, at one time, that we would never make it. Now, I really didn't know. Billy should have listened to the weather reporter. I began to worry because the telephone wouldn't work, and the lights were off. I began to cry and pray. I knew that was the only way I could find comfort.

It poured down raining for hours. Water was all over the restaurant. It began to come up to our knees. I was scared. We all sat on top of the tables to stand clear of the water. That was a real disaster. I will never forget it. I'm happy we all made it.

The sun was going down, and it was getting dark. On top of that, we had no lights. Everyone was afraid to go outside because glass and large boards from the other buildings were flying everywhere. The restaurant was so dark. We lit candles, but the wind kept blowing out the flames. By this time, half of the roof had blown off. We then moved to the backside where we could get out of the rain and wind, but we couldn't find a dry spot.

At approximately 9 p.m., the supervisor sent a big truck for us to move anyone or anything. We all were so happy to see that truck and started crying and running to get inside of it.

I MISSED THE BALL TEAM

All the restaurants had a ball team—baseball and basketball. Every first Sunday of the month, they would play against each other. It was fun. We'd gather food and drinks and go to the park. We could bring our friends if we liked. We had lots of food, compliments of Lathan's.

Most of our team was gay men, so the other team was made up of straight men. They treated our team like ladies, and they would laugh anytime guys on our team fell down. We had three Black guys on our team who were gay. Any one of them who felt slighted would curse at guys on the other team. Everyone would laugh as he switched away after telling the other guys off. It didn't seem to bother the white guys, but the Black guys would curse and try to fight. They couldn't handle the names the other team called them.

The other team would yell, "Where is your Vaseline? You need greasing!" And their teammates would laugh.

On Sunday we went to Bear Creek Park to play. It was a huge park. You could fish, play golf, tennis, bar-b-que, or anything you wanted to do. I thought everyone was having fun. There was a dance contest going on with a disc jockey playing music. We were eating and laughing, when one of the straight guys announced, "Now if you drop something, don't stoop over to pick it up—we have company!"

The next thing I knew, bottles were flying, and food was airborne. The gays started a fight, and everyone joined in. I ran and got into my car when I realized I couldn't stop them. The supervisor and managers were getting clobbered, and I knew why. They gays had it in for them already, and when the fight started, the managers got hit first. I looked around; Andy wasn't fighting. He was spraying whipped cream on everyone and laughing. They were all on cocaine.

The game, of course, was over. They were all draggy and bloody. Some were fired on the spot, and some weren't. It was a mess. I went home. I knew I would never follow them again. The next day at work, the guys were sore from fighting. They had Band-aids on their faces and arms.

Andy said, "We want to do that again sometime."

"What?" I said with a confused look on my face.

"We like to fight straight men. That turns us on! I love it." He licked his lips, and went on to say, "They're so masculine, and their muscles are so big. I just love when they hit me."

Then I knew why they'd started a fight with the other team. They enjoyed it. They were full of cocaine and couldn't feel anything. They were turned on. They liked men to beat them.

I was learning more and more about gays—how they thought and how they lived. They were sick in many ways. I knew they couldn't change the way they lived, so they made the best of it. I was more sad than happy around them. I learned that they were talented and smart. They could do almost anything. Hairdressers, musicians, cooks, decorator—they were talented.

I was invited to Andy's home for dinner. He really wanted me to see how he decorated his house. He lived with his lover Bill. Bill was the man, and Andy was the lady. Andy's home was beautiful. Every room was clean, walls painted with paper trimming at the top with the same color as the room. One room was totally green with paper trimming to match. The carpet was teal green, and the walls were white. All over the house were open windows. I couldn't understand why there weren't any curtains on any of the windows. I asked Andy about it, and he said, "When we walk through the house nude, people can see us." He never used curtains.

In the kitchen, the table was set. It was a beautiful mahogany table with high-back chairs. The table setting for eight on the table remained day in and day out. Andy had silverware from Tiffany's, each piece costing $55.00. Andy said he bought it once piece at a time from his tips at the restaurant. His tablecloth was white linen that he said Bill brought back from Paris. His bathroom had swans on the wall. This room was decorated in silver. The wallpaper was silver too—very pretty. The floor was grey tile. The shower curtain was grey, but it was cloth, and he had swan soaps on the dressing table. The ceiling was a glass mirror, with swans in the design.

I was shocked to see two men live with such elegance. Bill played the role of a man, and Andy played the woman. Bill took out the garbage and cut the grass, and Andy shopped and cooked. They both did laundry. Andy fixed Bill's plate and gave him the newspaper and his house slippers. Bill paid all the expenses. They were very organized—more than most male-female couples. They went to movies, the park, and night clubs together. If they had a problem, they'd sit down and talk about it. They were like husband and wife.

I enjoyed my visit to Andy's home. He was so nice to me. I believe he really loved me as his Mama. He always called me Mama. And I loved him like my son.

Several months after my visit, Bill was tested for HIV. He turned out to have AIDS. Andy was devastated and came to work crying and raving. All the waiters and waitresses tried to talk to him. He was so hurt. He knew this meant death for Bill since there was no cure for AIDS. There was nothing anyone could do except sit and wait for their loved one to die.

He kept asking, "Why Bill? He's so good to everyone. Why him?"

I had no answers for him.

He finally calmed down and tried to work, but he wasn't the same. He was worried about Bill. After lunch was over at the restaurant, the gays usually performed. They'd change into women's clothes, and they would dance on the tables. They'd clown. This was usually a lively everyday routine, but now it was dull and sad. The restaurant wasn't the same. The good times we'd had were over. The manager started hiring new help after everyone had died of AIDS.

This time he hired mostly young girls. Janet was the first of these. She was a Marilyn Monroe look-a-like. She had short blonde hair and wore red lipstick and nail polish. She walked like Marilyn Monroe, and all the kids told her she looked like Marilyn. She worked hard, and was friendly with everyone, especially Andy. She was stuck on him. She asked me all about him.

Finally, she smiled and said, "He's really cute. Does he like any of the other girls?"

"Ask Andy yourself," I said with a smirk. "He'll tell you what he likes."

He was very polite to her. Just because he would get her tray ready with water and bread and butter when he was caught up with his own tables, she thought he was attracted to her. I wasn't about to tell her he was gay. I told her to go try since he wasn't married. And she did. She often tried to kiss him, though he blocked her kisses with his hands. She started to be more serious and flirted with him every chance she got. Andy never told her the truth. They'd sit, eat lunch, laugh and play. They really had fun together.

One day Andy came to work dressed like Marilyn Monroe; this is just something he did. After work he'd cross dress and dance on stage like Marilyn Monroe.

Janet was left with her mouth open. She was shocked that Andy was gay. She really loved him. Andy had his makeup on better than Janet did. He really looked like Marilyn.

Janet didn't want to be outdone, so she talked to Pete, who was bi-sexual. He liked both girls and boys, so Janet and Pete started to date. She really cared for Pete. She'd talk about him at lunchtime. They went out often and engaged in sexual acts together with other people. She was just as wild as Pete. I thought she was a nice girl. Pete told me that Janet was also bi-sexual, so he had no problem. They were alike.

Three months later, Janet came to work very upset.

She said, "Mama, we have to talk. After lunch we must talk."

Her face was red and flushed. I knew something was wrong. I just didn't know what. I was trying hard to finish lunch, so I could find out what was going on.

Soon lunch was over, and we went into the Fifties Room, where we ate every day.

Janet sat down with me and said, "I'm pregnant, but I can't afford to have this baby. In fact, I don't know whose baby it is."

"You are dating Pete, aren't you?"

"Yes," she said. "But we have orgies, so I don't know who made me pregnant. Do you know where I can get help for free? I don't have the money to abort it, and Pete doesn't have the money saved up. I have no insurance. What am I going to do?" she cried. "I can't have a baby," she sobbed. "I will lose my figure and everything. I won't be able to pay my bills."

I knew that I'd worked at Lathan's long enough to get a loan. I also knew that Janet was in a very fragile emotional state. I could tell from how she talked that she would try to kill himself if someone didn't help her.

The next day, I asked her how much money she'd need, and she said, "Five hundred dollars."

"Give me a few days," I told her. "and I'll have the money."

Andy heard about what was going on. Pete told him, and he came to me to ask me if it was true. I told him what happened.

"We'll all help," he said. "We'll take up an offering for Janet, and all we can't raise, you can borrow."

But the kids pitched in enough that I didn't have to. Janet went to the clinic. They called her baby the Lathan's Baby because everyone pitched in to help after she aborted.

She was very happy. She was out on the floor laughing and waiting tables and walking like Marilyn Monroe again.

Pete left the restaurant and got a job dancing at night. He was a male stripper. He was making more money, and he said he could meet more men this way. He really cared more for men than women, but he wanted his father to think he liked girls too.

He said his father had tried to kill him when he was fifteen because Pete had been caught in the bathroom taking a bath with another boy. His dad walked in and saw them hugging and kissing. His dad screamed, and beat him. Pete got out of the tub and ran to his room. He told his dad he was just playing around; he didn't like boys. His dad didn't believe it.

Pete started to cry when he said, "My dad never hugged me again. In fact, he never touched me. I wanted him to be proud of me. But he never really talked to me again." He said later, "If my father would just take me in his arms and pat me on my back and say that everything's all right, I'd be happy, but he'd never do that. He shut me out. I can't reach him. But I love him."

I had no answer then either.

LEONARD'S LAST DAYS

Leonard was a very rich man. He had all the businesses in the River Oaks area and could decorate anything. He was a good man. I was glad to be his friend. He and his lover were very tall, about 6'3", and even looked alike. They both wore short, blonde hair. I could tell that something was wrong with Leonard. At the ball game on Sunday's, when Lathan's had a baseball team, once a month the stores played against each other. It was fun.

Leonard came to the game on warm days. Every time he came, he wore a heavy coat. I thought it was a strange but didn't say anything. His skin was very white when he had formerly been tanned all the time. I didn't have to wonder long. Andy came, sat down beside me, and started ringing his hands together, so I knew he was nervous.

I asked, "What's wrong?"

"Nothing," he answered. He shifted his hands then asked me, "What makes you think you know me that well?"

"I do know you and your ways, especially when something's wrong."

He began to cry while saying, "Leonard is leaving for Spain in the morning. He has AIDS."

"What?" I said loudly. "Are you sure? How long have you two known?"

We both cried. Andy said not to cry as he wiped his tears.

"He's known for three years. It's just getting bad now, so he's going to sell the flower shop and move to Spain."

Andy chose to stay here because he doesn't want to watch Leonard die.

"There is never anything we can do to help them." Then he cried even louder. "Mama, what am I going to do without my friends? They're all dying."

I reached out to him, but I couldn't stop the pain. It was true that every week some of his friends died of AIDS.

The next day at work, everyone talked about AIDS and what they were going to do. The medicine was too expensive to buy. There wasn't really any cure for AIDS. The AIDS clinic or hospital had closed down, and AIDS victims had no place to go.

Andy said, "I feel so isolated on this earth. I wish I could die."

I told him not to talk like that. "Keep hope alive, don't ever lose hope," I encouraged him. "Something will happen soon. They'll find a cure for AIDS."

I knew in my mind that wasn't true, but I didn't want him to lose all hope to live.

The following week was election time, and one of the candidates, Louie Welch, said on TV, "Shoot all gays."

Everyone at the restaurant was hurt; they cried and cried.

I announced right then and there, "We'll march against Louie Welch. He won't be the Mayor of this town."

Everyone was furious. We made flags and banners. On the 17th of August 1978, we marched, and Louis Welch lost to Kathy Whitmire. She won because she supported gay rights. After she became mayor, Andy and I made an appointment to meet with her to tell her the problems with the AIDS epidemic, and how so many were dying and had no money or jobs or insurance. After waiting for two months, we got an appointment with her and a small group of gays.

The meeting was very successful. The city funded an organization called the Houston AIDS foundation, and Mayor Whitmire made arrangements for gays to get free services there. Andy was so happy. He said, "Maybe all of my friends won't die. They made appointments right away to get tested." Out of six gays from the restaurant, four had HIV. Andy and Juan tested negative at the time.

ALLEN JONES, AND HOW
I LEFT THE CAFÉ

had been at Lathan's Café for six years, while managers had come and gone. However, there had never been a Black manager at the restaurant. Allen Jones was the first. He was from Mississippi. Mr. Jones was not a very handsome man. His hair was sliding off the back of his head. That left more face to see. He had "popped" eyes. I mean, they were protruding out of his head. He was ugly. When we met, he wasn't as friendly as the previous managers. Actually, he wasn't friendly at all! I thought we would work together really well, but I was wrong.

On Mr. Jones' first day, he changed all of the rules. In fact, he created rules because we basically had none. Before he came to Lathan's, we were all like one big family. Everyone knew what to do and how to do it. In essence, we worked very well together. Nevertheless, Mr. Jones communicated his own rules.

"<u>Rule number 1</u>: Everyone has to call me Mr. Jones."

We laughed at this rule, but Mr. Jones didn't laugh at all. The staff could not stop laughing although Mr. Jones was very serious.

"<u>Rule number 2</u>: "I don't like gays."

I thought that was rude for him to say. Everyone knew where they stood with him based on this statement.

He looked at me and said, "I hear everyone calls you 'mama.'" He then said, "I wouldn't let them call me 'mama' if I were you."

I looked at him for a long period of time. I was trying to find the right words to say without hurting his feelings, but I couldn't find any.

Finally, I told him "We all know that I am not their mother, but this is their way of showing respect and love for me. So, I don't mind if they call me 'mama.'"

Mr. Jones then put his head down and walked away. Everyone was angry at him. They said, "He can't come here and change things; that's not fair." Andy and Ivan were angry because Mr. Jones said that he didn't like gays. In spite of how we felt about Mr. Jones and his unfair rules, we still had to work with him. He was our new manager. I made up my mind that I was going to try hard to work with him. I couldn't understand why he was so rude and didn't like gays. They are people and have feelings like everyone else.

One day, Mr. Jones met me in the dining room area and said, "Let's talk."

I stopped and looked at him.

"Let's talk one on one," he said.

"Okay, what do you want to talk about?"

"Your job," he said while he pulled one of the chairs and motioned for me to sit.

I sat, and so did he.

"You have been here for ten years, and I think you are getting too old for this job. Mostly school kids work in a restaurant for minimum wages, and you are as high as you can go unless you become a manager. You don't have any degrees for that. So, I suggest you take a vacation. When you come back, we will work out something for you."

I was happy to take a vacation. I really needed the rest. So, I thanked him and shook his hand for the first time. I thought that Mr. Jones was not too bad.

I told Andy that I was going on a two-week vacation. He was happy for me. We began to talk about places to go and how much it would cost. This was a good time to take a vacation.

At the end of the week, I left for Las Vegas. I was there for three days when I called back to talk to Andy and my children. I was having fun. I had never been to Vegas before. This was all new to me.

When I talked to Andy, he told me that Mr. Jones had fired Ivan and Pete because they were approximately 10 minutes late coming to work. Andy was very upset.

"He just wanted to fire them," Andy said accusingly. "He wants to get rid of all the gay guys, and he sent you away so that he could fire everybody."

I was shocked. I didn't know what to say.

Andy went on to say, "I may not be here when you get back. The secretary has left too."

"Oh my God! What is going on?" I said.

I couldn't figure out. I was confused but continued thinking about the whole situation. I then began to understand why Mr. Jones wanted to talk to me about my job. When I returned from my vacation, I wouldn't have a job either. I was supposed to return Sunday.

I made up my mind to forget about work for the time being and enjoy the rest of my time off, and I did just that. I really did have fun in Vegas.

I called Andy when I got home; and we talked for hours about Allen Jones. We talked about how he made everyone pay for their lunch although we ate free for years. He had changed everything. We couldn't sit in the back room anymore. We had to sit up front. We couldn't play and have fun up front because he sat with us. Andy was furious. Mr. Jones tried to make everyone quit. He basically wanted a new staff.

He had heard about the gays, and he didn't like them. The supervisor told Mr. Jones to get rid of everyone and hire new people. We eventually figured this out.

Mr. Jones met me at the door when I got to work on Monday.

He said, "Let's talk. Your cooking job—I gave it to Dennis. I want you to start garnishing plates."

"What?" I said in a loud voice.

"Yes, you are getting too old for this job." He continued explaining in his very rude and forward manner, "I want someone younger to cook."

"I will not step down," I refused. "I garnished plates when I first started working here ten years ago, and I have been promoted to kitchen manager."

It was as if he heard nothing I had just said.

"Yes, by the way, give me your keys to the restaurant," He held out his hand for my keys.

I looked at him in disbelief. Not only was this man being ugly, but he was crazy. I ran to the office to call Carl, the supervisor, who previously told me to let him if I ever had any problems with a manager or employee. I called him. When he answered the phone, I was screaming and hollering. He couldn't understand me. He kept telling me to calm down so he could understand what I was saying. I couldn't. I couldn't believe this man, Jones, had demoted me back to garnishee. I tried to tell Carl, the supervisor, but I was too upset. I wasn't making sense to Carl, so he decided to come to the restaurant to talk to me.

I ran to the office to wait for Carl. I thought to myself, "Carl will fix everything." I couldn't stop crying. I also thought to myself that Carl would give Ivan and Pete back their jobs and give me back my position as kitchen manager. I then began to say to myself, "Hurry up, Carl, hurry up and get here so you can fix everything."

I began to reflect on how much of myself I had given to the restaurant. I thought of the times I had to open the restaurant by myself. When the manager was late, I would open the front door.

As my thoughts went from racing to a normal pace of thoughts, I connected the past to the present situation. I realized that I had recently run the very system now being used against me. It now made sense now to me. If the black man demotes me and replace me with a white boy, Carl wouldn't be accused of discrimination. They had it all figured out before Mr. Jones sent me on vacation. It was really termination.

I left and went home. I couldn't handle anymore. I had been betrayed by Carl, my friend—or who I thought was my friend.

The same night, Mr. Jones called me at home. He said, "We don't want you to leave. Please come and garnish the plates." I felt like he had slapped me in my face every time he said "garnish plates."

"I'll never go backwards," I responded. "If I can't go forward, please don't ask me to go backwards."

Mr. Jones told me that Carl was afraid of AIDS and that he wanted to get rid of all the gays. He explained, "Carl knows how much you care for the gays. As a result, he wants to get rid of you too."

I said, "That's just fine then. I will file on Lathan's Café for discrimination against me. You told me that I was too old for the job, and that is called discrimination."

Bright and early the next day, I went to the Equal Employment Opportunity Commission (EEOC) to file my complaint. I was sick inside from what Jones told me.

"I am too old for that job," I mumbled. "Humph! How dare he tell me that?" I thought to myself.

I was angry, hurt, and embarrassed. Although the kids were in their teens, I wasn't old. I was 36, and besides, I didn't feel old. I had been doing my work and others' too. Furthermore, I was always prompt and on time. He really had no right to tell me that. I had often been in charge of the whole restaurant when the manager was late, drunk or had a hangover. Now, I was considered too old.

I then decided, "I can't and won't let him get away with this—Never!"

I couldn't help it if they didn't like gay people or were afraid of catching AIDS. I had been reading about AIDS and how it was contracted:

1. Sex
2. Blood; and
3. Dirty Needles

I didn't worry about getting AIDS because I didn't do any of the above.

I thought to myself, "If the manager was smart, he'd know that he couldn't get AIDS from just being around people with AIDS."

When I filed on Lathan's Café for discrimination, I had to fill out so many forms. I was also asked an enormous amount of questions, but I stuck with it. I actually got disgusted with the whole process, but I stayed with it for two years. During that time, they investigated all Lathan's Café restaurants. I had been known as "Mama" at each one. Other employees from different Lathan's Café testified on my behalf. I received a lot of good reports. All of the kids that worked with me went to the EEOC and testified on my behalf. I had more than enough support.

Finally, I won. I could have gotten my job back with two years back pay. However, I just took the pay. Nursing was the area for which I had received training and work for years, but I wanted something different. As a result, I began working at Lathan's Café, which was a different experience for me. I decided to go back to nursing.

After I won at the EEOC, I didn't want my job back. I didn't want the company that meant so much to me to be forced to take me back. I wanted everything to be like it was. I had given so much of myself to Lathan's Café and to people that worked there that I didn't want to go through that again. I also realized that I had neglected my own family so many times. I had been with Lathan's Café family when I should have been with my family. I worked long evening hours and spent the rest of my time on the phone with some of the kids that worked there. I had given a lot of myself to the people. I later believed that they didn't need me anymore. Nevertheless, I often daydream about many things that happened at Lathan's Café when I worked there.

THE LAST OF ANDY

Andy was the last one to get HIV. He was afraid he'd get it. He changed his lifestyle by staying at home, not picking up strangers anymore, and changing his eating habits. He had really changed. He tried to take care of himself, but it was too late. He had HIV.

Although he would eat and eat, he lost weight every week. He talked about his friends, how he hated to see them since they were all skin and bones, dying from full-blown AIDS.

He cried when he talked about how his lover Bill looked when he died. "Mama," he said. "If I hadn't known that was Bill, I wouldn't have believed it! He was grey and looked like he was 90 years old! I don't want to die, please, God, don't let me die!"

I felt helpless. All my kids were dying of AIDS, and there was nothing I could do. There was no cure for it.

As time went on, Andy was doing fine. He had slowed down a lot. He didn't have AIDS yet, so he started working at Bill's flower shop. He'd eat half gallons of ice cream every day, so he wouldn't lose weight.

He was trying with all his might to hold on, but he knew it was just a matter of time.

He would call me every day to talk about old times. Before he hung up, he'd ask me to pray for him, and I would. It wasn't easy for me. Every time one of the kids would die, I felt like something was taken away from me. I loved those kids! I knew in my heart I'd done my best. I told them the truth, but I couldn't change their lives.

A year went by. I hadn't seen Andy. He called every day, but I had not seen him. So, he wanted to see me.

He said, "Mama, I have to see you. I don't want to leave this world and not see you."

So, we met at the Warwick for lunch.

He brought me an apple and said, "This is for you." I hugged him and thanked him. He said, "Apples bring your blood pressure down, so eat an apple every day."

I agreed and said I would. We sat down for lunch. His face was full of sores—his arms too. He tried to smile. He still had the same smile, but his spirits were low. He was pushing himself for me. He wanted me to think he was fine, the way he'd always done, but I knew he was in pain.

I could hardly eat, so at last I said, "I have to leave to pick up my grandson from school."

I left in a hurry. It hurt me to see him that way, so I had to leave.

I cried all the way home. He was just like my own child. I really loved Andy. He was a true friend. I never saw Andy again.

Two weeks later, I received a letter from Andy, who now knew he was dying, it read:

Dear Mama,

I really don't want to leave you, although I have no choice. Will you please forgive me? I've been very bad—do you think God will forgive me? I never hurt anyone, except myself, and my parents. I want my parents to forgive me too. I love them, but they never loved me back, but you did—you didn't hate me because I'm gay. You showed me love I never knew existed before.

Thanks Mama—thanks for everything. I don't have anything to leave you. I haven't worked for two years. I used all my funds, I've pawned all my jewelry for medicine, and all I can leave you is memories of the times we shared together. Mama, when you pray to God, tell him I'm sorry.

Andy

MEMORIES

The hardest thing for me was to watch the kids die from AIDS. Their bodies were full of sores, and they lost so much weight that all the fun we had together was over. They were so depressed, and their spirits so low that I hated to visit them in the hospital. I would still carry them fruit and candies. I tried to fatten them up, but I knew it was hopeless. Their lives were over.

They were so young to die before they had ever even lived. What a shame. I often thought to myself. I would get their parents' addresses and write to tell them that their child was dying. They'd answer and say, "My child was already dead. He died the day he turned gay."

I didn't know what to say to the kids when they would ask if their parents had answered. I'd say, "Not yet." I didn't want to tell them that their parents didn't care. I couldn't tell them the truth. God knows I wanted to have a good answer for them, but I couldn't. Their pain was unbearable—to be rejected by society, as well as their family.

From 1982 to 1992, all the kids at the café who were gay died, except Andy. He was the only one living. He gained weight and started living with another lover. His other lover died from AIDS. It didn't seem to bother Andy, who went on with his life working at a flower shop in the Galleria area. I visited him often just to see if he was okay and to see that he was still free from AIDS.

I have so many fond memories of Lathan's Café. Sometimes I get depressed thinking about it. For five years, I went to counseling to get my life back together. Before, I would sit and cry for no reason. If only I could have been able to persuade the kids from Lathan's Café to seek God in their lifetime, because Jesus is the answer. I finally realized that I was feeling guilty for something I had no control over—and that was other people's choices.

Although doctors say there is no cure, I continue to witness people with AIDS live without pain and symptoms of the illness. In some cases, the doctors don't understand why HIV virus has not turned into AIDS. In 1992-1993, more and more people lived longer because they turned to Jesus. The ones who did not believe me died from AIDS.

Looking back at it all, it seems like a dream. It seems like none of this really happened. We were friends, and we loved each other. What happened? Before I knew it, it was over. The fun at the restaurant was all over.

The few kids who survived the ordeal are still very close to me. We keep in touch with each other by phone. I haven't seen them in a while, but they are fine.

Since I joined the prayer group, I feel so much better. I attend prayer once a week. We pray at noon every day for everyone, especially people with AIDS.

We pray that AIDS will not destroy another generation.

ABOUT THE AUTHOR

Charlene Latham (Mama) was born in Eagle Lake, Texas. She moved to Houston in 1957, where she married James Lathan and became the proud mother of three daughters and one son. She has been a faithful member of Mt. Hebron Missionary Baptist Church since 1960. She went to nursing school at St. Philip Nursing School in San Antonio, Texas, and has worked in the medical field for over thirty years. She writes life changing books and plays in her spare time.